DISAPPEARING
LIKE THE
WIND

BOB KILLINGER

Foreword by Mark Day

Have fun
+
God Bless!
Bo S-o

For all my buddies at Houston Oaks Country Club,
and my muni-brothers at Memorial Park and Sharpstown.
Thanks for the great times we've had,
and I look forward to the great times to come.

FOREWORD

This is a great story by a natural storyteller.

I first met Bob Killinger at Houston Oaks Country Club in 2015 when Olympian Liezel Huber was establishing the tennis program there. Bob was working on his game with a view toward winning the club championship (he did), and I was trying to find something to do after my semi-successful triathlon career was over (I didn't).

The first thing I learned about Bob was that he started his own successful company as a twelve-year-old boy by trademarking the phrase "If God isn't a Longhorn, why's the sunset burnt orange?" and selling thousands upon thousands of bumper stickers to loyal alumni and fans of The University of Texas.

We hit it off and started meeting for the occasional lunch or breakfast, and I found that I did little of the talking—and that was quite fine—because Bob had many more stories than I did, and they were quite a bit more interesting than mine. Stories like:

His success as a walk-on on the #1 ranked NCAA men's soccer team at the University of North Carolina

- His pro soccer career

- His pro golf career

- His conversation with OJ Simpson

- His dance with Phyllis Diller at the Petroleum Club

- His singing lessons at the Houston Grand Opera, and his days of playing the ukulele and singing in front of the local Home Depot

- How his grandfather invented the Koozie (called "Killinger Koozies," and some still exist)

As with most proud fathers, our conversations often swing to his three children, Jordan, William, and Caroline, and to his lovely wife, Elizabeth, who is a captain of industry in Houston, and they are all quite remarkable in their own right.

One of his stories was about a book he had written years ago and how one gets a book published. He let me read the book (this isn't it), and I was pleased, but not surprised, as to how good it was.

He later told me about another book he planned to write (this book), and the plot sounded like a movie waiting to happen. I have been Bob's guinea pig on this book—reading it chapter by chapter as he cranked out the pages, and I found myself pushing him for each new installment.

While I am not a literary critic, I read quite a bit for both business and pleasure, and I can confirm that this book is not the work of a first-timer or an amateur. In truth and in fact, it's a bit of a page-turner.

Don't let the cover fool you. This is not a book about golf. While golfers will undoubtedly enjoy finding the links sections to be technically accurate and situationally plausible, non-golfers will find these parts to be completely understandable, engaging, and compelling.

As they say on the golf course, "You're up!"

Mark Day
Houston, Texas
January 4, 2018

Chapter 1

Through Her Eyes

It was his hands. As a child, I never understood why his swing was so lauded and admired, but now, with twenty years of playing under my belt, I finally appreciated why he was such a phenomenon. His hands knew how to hit a golf ball. They were born knowing, with a grasp of not only how to hold the club but also how to create an angle of approach that leads to a consistency of contact beyond my comprehension.

His hands led him to develop his unconventional swing, and unconventional was an understatement. His foot positions changed with each pass of the club, like a spontaneous dance with the golf ball. By manipulating his feet, he could hit it high, low, fade, draw, in a way only he could pull off because his hands always got him back to perfect position at impact, and the sound when he struck a golf ball was primal, shocking, like a charismatic mixture of hostility and precision. If you love golf, you marveled at the smooth rhythm of his takeaway, the effortless transition at the top, then the mighty thrust through impact, ending with his trademark exaggerated finish. Watching him now, it was almost ethereal, with the orange-tinged Texas sunrise gently glowing through the pine trees in the distance.

But he didn't respect or care about his swing. He never did. Travis was almost embarrassed by it all.

I've never met a human being with more gifts who acted like he didn't want them. A handsome man, with unexpected deep blue eyes, taller than average, and born with a six-pack, even in his early sixties now. A smart guy, but he resisted flaunting it, almost hoping not to show it, or maybe not wanting to be expected to use it in life. Always approachable, with an endearing smile. Travis was simply the finest, most beloved golfer that the Houston municipal golf world had ever known.

Watching him on the driving range, it brought back my memories of being a little girl and getting weekly lessons from this legend, starting over two decades ago. Crowds would gather trying to eavesdrop on the golf secrets Travis taught me, and I was known as *'Travis's little girl.'* God, I loved him. When I lost my father at age six, Travis took over for him. Whenever it was Special Visitor's Day at school or field day, or I just needed someone to talk to, he was always there for me. If Travis's family went on a trip, I tagged along. His two daughters were about the same age as me, but we weren't close. I think they were jealous of Travis and me. His daughters never played golf, both were more into academics than sports, and there was always a little distance between them and Travis. Their kindred relationship was always awkward, and I think Travis liked using me as a buffer between them.

He caddied for me in my high school golf tournaments, carrying me to ten amateur wins, and also helping me obtain a golf scholarship from Duke University. One phone call from Travis was all it took for my scholarship. He wouldn't let me go anywhere else, said I'd be safe there. With that one phone call, Travis gave me the opportunity to receive one of the best educations in the country, and the ability to build an extraordinary life, a life with options, more options than I deserved with my under-achieving grades. He never wanted a thank you, just wanted me to be safe.

Travis loved me, and he changed my life many times, always for the better.

But we lost touch over the years. I got busy in college and then in the working world, and when both his daughters left for college, it was almost like Travis dropped out for a while, traveling randomly across the country, I'm not sure why. I stopped calling, feeling like he needed his space.

I flew into Houston yesterday morning, the first time back in six years, to visit my mother for a couple of days was the stated excuse. A few days before, I called Memorial Park Golf Course, talked to the head pro, Glenn, and asked him about Travis. He said Travis was back and living in Houston again, and that Travis played Memorial Park every morning. Walking here from an unknown residence, Travis would hit a few practice balls on the range at around 6:00 am, then he played the back nine alone. Glenn said that if you weren't watching for him, you'd probably miss him.

Typical Travis. He does everything alone.

So I got to the Memorial Park early this morning and watched as my mentor slowly came into view, walking with a carry bag over his shoulders, golf shoes on his feet, heading for the far end of the range. Practice balls were already poured out for him by the grounds crew, and after some minor stretching, he began his familiar warm up. There was a bench near his stall, so I snuck up and sat right down, quietly appreciating this moment in time, but I couldn't take it any longer.

Chapter 2

─────◆─────

Coming Home

"That's the ugliest swing I've ever seen."

A little startled, Travis turned with a fake smile, probably thinking it was a sarcastic fan, then looked blown away. "Ava?"

"You got it, old man," she said, walking over, then giving him a big hug.

"Oh my God. Did you graduate?"

"Sure did," she answered, giving one last big squeeze before letting go. "Five years ago. Last in my class, probably."

"You are such a lazy ass. What's your degree in?"

"Communications."

"Perfect," Travis laughed, placing his seven iron back in the golf bag. "The only thing you could ever do was talk. Now at least you have a degree in it. So what do you do with a communications degree, champ?"

"I wanted to be a sportscaster."

"Wanted?"

"I just quit a broadcasting job in Connecticut and flew back to Houston for a couple of days, to visit Mom. I figured you never had a job so why should I? Maybe I can be your caddy now."

"Oh, Jesus, Ava," Travis grinned. "Your mother must hate me. Please tell me you don't say stuff like that around her."

"She doesn't care. Mom got married again, so I'm old news. I'm staying in the '*outside bungalow*' of their mansion. It's so weird for her to be rich now. She even talks differently."

"Good for her."

"By the way, did you walk here? Where the hell do you live?"

"Dumpster #7, by the tennis courts," he answered wryly.

"Hey Travis, how's it going, brother?" a random guy yelled from across the parking lot. "We love you, man, and screw everybody else!"

Travis put on a plastic smile and gave him a thumbs-up. "I better tee off. Golfers are starting to arrive now." He slipped the golf bag over his shoulder. "Hey, you want to ride with me while I play the back nine? Or, hey, do you have your clubs? Join me."

"My sticks are in Connecticut, but I'd love to hang out with you."

They headed toward a cart on the other side of the range.

"You don't pay for practice balls, or a cart, or your golf," Ava said. "They just put everything out for you. No wonder you don't have a job."

"Just get in, Miss Communications."

The course was as beautiful as ever, Houston's municipal golfing diamond. One of the oldest and most revered courses in Texas, Memorial Park had been the home to many of Houston's most celebrated golfers, like Jimmy Demaret and Doug Sanders. A long golf course, mostly straight, with deep penalizing rough and bumpy-slick greens, it was the home for all the major amateur competitions for the city, and from 1951 through 1963, was the site for The Houston Open, where the great Arnold Palmer won in 1957. Of course, there were more expensive and exclusive clubs in Houston, with better playing conditions and fresher designs, but Memorial Park was the Mecca for Houston golfers, and the only place someone like Travis would call home. As we drove toward the tenth tee, I almost felt like saying a prayer.

"Do you get to play much anymore?" Travis asked as he pushed down hard, trying to tee his golf ball in the baked Texas ground.

"Not really. Seventy-hour workweeks didn't give me much of a chance. And I needed a break from golf, also. Duke golf kinda' burned me out and the game wasn't as much fun anymore. Work became more fulfilling than golf, you know what I mean? I haven't picked up the sticks in almost six months."

"You're just growing up, kid," he said, beginning his swing, then pounding it down the right side of the fairway, a slight draw, teasing a fairway trap ever so gently, then the ball skipped down the middle, about 310 yards. "You were always too smart for your age, and I knew you couldn't play a game your entire life. You get bored too easily, and you like meaningful challenges. I'm just proud of you for playing golf long enough to get your degree. I'm sure you're an amazing young woman now."

"Thanks," Ava said. "I was a little scared to tell you that I wasn't playing anymore. I loved it as a kid, and hanging out with you was the greatest time of my life. But I guess—." She composed herself. "Well, I guess that I finally realized that I could never be you."

"Oh, Ava," Travis said, getting out of the cart, studying his next shot. He pulled out an iron, lined it up, then gently launched it skyward, the ball landing dead center of the green. "You will always be better than me."

"No, I'm not. Especially not at golf. I look back now and realize how amazing you were, how you convinced me that I was a great golfer and that I could do anything on a golf course. I won golf tournaments in high school because you convinced me that I could, walking with me and telling me that I was a badass. But I got to college and they all hit it further, hit it cleaner, and I learned that I couldn't read greens without you. I'm not a great golfer. I'm just a woman who knows how to play golf, who knows a guy who is a golfing genius, and he got me a golfing scholarship that I didn't deserve."

Travis looked the other way, trying to find the words, then stopped the cart by the green.

"You earned that scholarship, Ava."

He walked onto the green, fixed his pitch mark and picked up his ball, not wanting to putt but concentrate on Ava.

As he walked back, Travis explained, "I got a call from the Duke golf coach decades ago, way before you graduated from high school. He heard about me through a friend and wanted me to talk to a recruit for him, a Houston girl, as a favor, to help the girl understand that Duke wasn't New York City, and how prestigious this opportunity was for her. I did it, and she went to Duke. He called me three more times through the years, and all three of those girls went also.

"So your senior year of high school, your mom had no money for college, and your grades were mediocre at best. I called the Duke coach and said it was time for him to return the favor. He agreed and happily offered you the scholarship." Travis sat back down in the cart. "You earned that scholarship. You've been there for me my whole life."

"Oh, Travis," Ava said, shaking her head. "All I've ever done is take from y—."

"That's a bunch of bull," Travis interrupted. "When I needed a caddy, you were there. When my wife died, you were the first person to call me and ask if I was ok. You were a six-year-old kid when you called to check on me. You've been there for me through thick and thin, no questions asked. You made me understand that life is worth living again. So you did, yes, you did earn that scholarship. Maybe not for golf. But for everything that you did for me. It was all that I could give you. You earned it."

"Oh, you bastard," Ava said, wiping away a few tears. "Here I am, trying to tell you how I let you down, but you make me into some fake hero. Don't you ever stop?"

Travis pulled the cart under the shade of an oak tree.

"So why did you come home?"

Ava sighed, "I needed a break. Life got complicated, and I just wanted to slow down."

"Are you in love with some guy?"

"What the hell, Travis?" Ava asked, shaking her head in amazement. "Is there a sign on my back?"

"Just makes sense," he answered. "You haven't been home in ages. What, he can't afford a ring?"

"I haven't said 'Yes' yet. I asked for some time to think it over."

"Wait. Let me get this straight. You quit your job so you could figure out if you want to get married?"

"No. He popped the question after I quit."

"Wow, brave man," Travis laughed. "He must really love you, or is he completely insane?"

"Oh, I don't know," she blurted out, her head in her hands now. "He's great, but I'm not."

"What's wrong, kiddo?" he asked, leaning back in the cart.

"I don't know what I want to do in life. He has it all under control. And I don't want to screw up his life. I could end up being my mom, and he'll hate me."

"Ava, have you ever been arrested?"

"No."

"Are you a drunk, or do drugs?"

"No, of course not."

"So you're not a criminal, and you don't do drugs. You've never had a child out of wedlock, as far as I know. You are a little bit of a germophobe, but that's no big deal. You're the opposite of a feminist, thank God. So what's so wrong with you?"

"Everything."

Travis laughed, then looked right into her eyes.

"You are one of the funniest people on earth. Your smile lights up any room. Whether you like it or not, you're a good-looking woman, just like your mother. You are loyal, a good friend, and the kind of person that everyone wants in their life. You are almost the perfect wife, a partner that any man would die for in their life. This guy would be lucky to have you. So what makes him so great?"

Ava took a deep breath.

"He's an orthopedic surgeon, a deacon in our church, mentors foster children in his spare time; he's gorgeous, and he adores me. Also, he's a damn fine golfer."

Travis gently leaned back in the cart again.

"Does he ever date older men?"

They busted out laughing, Ava cackling now.

"Why me? Why would a man like that want to spend the rest of his life with me? I'll be a constant weight in his life."

"No, darling, you're the missing piece," Travis answered, nodding his head. "A man like that needs a woman who he can trust and respect, that won't abuse the privilege of being his spouse. He needs a woman who respects what he does and won't expect him to become someone else as the years go on. He needs an independent woman who can take care of herself, and has her own goals that he can help her fulfill." Travis stared at her again. "If you don't love him, then let him go. You will be wasting both your lives." He grabbed her hand now. "But if you do love him, go for it, help make both your dreams come true and have the life that y'all deserve. You've had some roadblocks and heartbreaks, and you've come through them like a champion. You deserve to be happy. It sounds like you both deserve to be happy."

Struggling not to break down, she reached over and hugged him, long and hard.

"I love him, Travis. Oh, I adore him. I hope he loves me. I think he does. I can't believe it, but I think he really does."

"I trust you and your instincts," Travis answered. "I'd bet my life on your instincts."

"Stop it, damn it. Stop being my caddy. You make me miss golfing with you."

"I can't help it. You're the best, and it's the truth. And I'm so happy for you. You're going to have a wonderful life, and you deserve it. Why don't you call him right now and give him the good news? Then we can celebrate. I know the perfect place."

Chapter 3

The Reason

"Oh, my God," she gushed, her mouth full of the greasy burger, "how can it still taste this good?"

"Whataburger never lets you down," Travis answered, dipping an onion ring in the spicy ketchup. "Maybe you can serve it at the rehearsal dinner. Or does your Yankee doctor only eat kale and quiche?"

"Screw you," she smirked. "There's nothing wrong with eating healthy. And Richie likes ice cream, so hah! And how do you still eat this stuff and have a flat belly? I'd never fit in a wedding dress if I lived here."

"I'm bulimic. By the way, where is the bathroom?"

"Shut up!" she laughed, cackling again. "Seriously though, thanks for saying '*Hi*' to my Richie. He's a huge fan and ecstatic now. I can hear him right now, telling everybody at the hospital about the phone call and how he talked to Travis Hatfield. I know he's jealous that you're going to walk me down the aisle and not him."

"Whoa. Wait a minute. I don't walk you down the aisle. What about your stepdad?"

Ava put down her burger, sternly.

"I've met him only three times in my life, Travis, including Mom's wedding, and he didn't even go to the airport with Mom to pick me up yesterday. He stayed home to watch TV. Judge Judy."

"Oh, Ava."

"Hey," she said, pointing at him, "you told me to marry Richie. You've got to walk me down the aisle now."

"I didn't tell you to marry a Yankee," Travis said weakly. He leaned back and thought to himself, almost pleading for a different answer, but none came. Taking a deep breath, then a loud exhale, he answered, "I'd be honored to walk you, but I don't have to wear a tux, right?"

"You'll look hot. Like James Bond. Agent Travis Hatfield Bond. And you have to bring a date."

He tried to smile, then slowly looked off away into the distance. They sat quietly and ate for a minute.

"Travis, I didn't come back to visit Mom."

"Oh, yeah?"

She measured her words carefully.

"I came back for you. I came back to help you."

Puzzled, yet concerned, he methodically responded, "Ava, I'm fine."

"Maybe. Maybe you are. But you need help." Ava leaned toward him, her elbows on the table now and a quieter voice. "Don't you wonder why I quit my job?"

"No. That's your business, and I figure you'd tell me if it was important. Most people quit a job in their twenties. It's part of growing up and learning who you are."

"I got into broadcasting at Duke," Ava began. "During the summer before my sophomore year, the football broadcast team wanted a sideline reporter, and being the trend right now, I guess they wanted a woman to be on the sidelines. I fit that criteria, so I became the Duke sideline reporter. I loved it, got pretty good at it, and by my senior year, I had my own weekend sports show on the Duke local access network.

"When I graduated, I tried to find a sportscasting gig, but unless you have a gold medal or you've rushed for 10,000 yards in the NFL, it's a tough job to find. I sent resumes everywhere and got almost no callbacks. So I went to work for a sports marketing company with the Carolina Panthers, having fun with friends and scraping by, waiting for my big break.

"Then I got a phone call from a small market station called Freedom Sports Network in Connecticut. It was a local sports channel dedicated to New England sports, from high school to the pros. I flew there the next day to interview.

"The interview didn't go very well at first. I knew almost nothing about New England sports, and my Texas accent was not appreciated. Right before the producer was going to kick me out of his office, he asked if I had anything interesting in my background sports-wise."

"You mentioned me," Travis added.

"Yeah." She took a sip of her diet coke. "He was early fifties, knew your story well, and hired me instantly. He helped me sign a lease at an apartment complex, a fantastic place with vaulted ceilings, and gave me a company car. My dream started coming true.

"The job went well at first. I was a runner and odd-jobs person, no airtime, but I was promised a shot in a few months. The hours were horrible, but I got to see and do some cool things.

"Anyway, after six months, a week ago, the producer asked to see me in his office. He offered me a promotion, a good one, almost twice my salary. There was one catch: I had to get an interview with you, discussing why you retired and the situation with your wife. Of course, I said no way. Then he said either I did the interview or I'm fired. The bastard even threatened me with the apartment lease, saying I would be stuck with it, a two-year lease.

"So I quit and walked out. I talked to the apartment people, and they let me out of the lease, no problem. They had another person ready to replace me. I don't have to move out officially for another 60 days, so I'm fine. I got lucky."

Travis tried to look her in the eyes.

"I'm sorry the job didn't work out."

"It's ok, Travis. I found out everything that I wanted to know about that world, and I know now that it's not for me, and I found out how much more I love Richie than being a sportscaster. It was a learning experience, and I'm better for it."

"Good girl."

"But," she sighed, "the whole situation in New England made me realize something. You see, I get asked about you all the time. Your story still lives on to this day. Hell, I'm the answer to a trivia question: what was the name of the little girl who caddied for Travis Hatfield at the Houston Open?"

"Ok," Travis answered, a little aggravated now. "Do you want me to apologize for that also?"

"No, I can deal with it. I always have. Proudly. But it is easy for me. Everyone smiles when they remember me as a little girl. People talk about how lucky I was and what a great experience I had. I don't get hurt by my relationship with you in any way. No one asks me about your marriage or your wife, and if they do, I can say '*I don't know*' and no one bothers me anymore."

"What are we talking about, Ava?"

She leaned in.

"Your daughters."

"Leave them out of this," Travis said, not amused.

"No," Ava said emphatically. "I realized that whatever troubles that I've had from being a part of your life, their troubles have been ten times worse than mine. I bet they get asked what happened to their mom every day and if you did it. It started to haunt me so bad, I went online to check on them a few days ago, and I read about what happened at SMU."

Travis grimaced, just staring out the window, wanting her to stop.

"Poor Charlotte was stalked at her dorm by reporters, constantly asking her about you and her mother. The poor thing had to drop out."

"She transferred," Travis corrected. "And she is fine now. The University of Missouri was a good school, and she did great."

"Travis, this has to end."

"How!" Travis blurted out, startling everyone in the burger joint. He lowered his voice and leaned forward. "Fine. I ruined their lives. It kills me, but I accept that. What the hell else can I do?"

"It's easy for you, Travis. You just hide away from life and surround yourself with people who worship you. But your daughters can't. They aren't beloved by everyone like you. They have no place to escape. Charlotte and Shelby are considered victims, or, worse, people who know the truth and are hiding something. No one thinks that I know anything, so I'm left alone. But everyone thinks your daughters know some dark, scary truth about you, and are hiding it to protect either you or themselves from you. Travis, you have to protect your daughters like you protect yourself in your own life. They need to be left alone."

Travis leaned back in his chair, crushed.

"I can't believe you think that I don't want to protect my children. I've done everything that I can."

"No, you haven't, Travis. You never told everyone the truth. People don't know what really happened." She leaned in again. "Travis, I don't know what really happened."

"You were six years old! You expected me to explain it to you?"

"But I'm 27 now," she said, gently, grabbing his hand. "You daughters are out of college and have their own lives, and they don't know what really happened, do they?"

"Ava," Travis said like a father, "they know all they need to know, and they are fine."

"They are terrorized by your story daily. Your daughters need your protection."

Travis shook his head in disgust.

"Has it ever occurred to you that I am protecting my family by not telling the world my story?"

Ava leaned back in her chair now, looking at him curiously, trying to make sense of his reasoning.

Then it hit her.

"You're protecting your wife. That's why this is best for your family."

"Everyone knows all they need to know. So just drop it."

Shocked by his logic, she was also relieved, realizing he was trying to be generous, like the Travis she had always known.

"This isn't fair, Travis."

"Life isn't fair, little girl. Trust me."

"This is wrong. You have taken too much of the blame."

"How do you know?" Travis responded. "And who cares? None of it matters anymore. They still love their mom in their own way, I hope. That is all that matters."

"But do they love you, Travis? Not the way that they should. They can't because they don't know what really happened. Don't they deserve to have a father that they can love also? Their mother is gone, but their father is still here. You're still here."

Travis put up his hands, pleading for this to end.

"I can't believe you're doing this to me."

"I want to help you, old man," she said, trying to make him smile.

"Well, you suck at it," he said, with a fake smile back.

"That's why I came to see you. I want to write your story. I want to help you get this horrible monkey off your back, and to help you protect your daughters. To finally repay you for all that you've done for me."

"Write my story? A stupid article or something. What the hell, Ava?"

"A novel," she corrected. "The whole story, written by someone that you know, that you can trust. I won't change your story or slander you and your family in anyway. All the sales will go to your daughters, or a foundation for your wife, or whatever. I don't care. I just want to help you and your daughters from this misery."

"Are you serious? It could be terrible. It could be one horrible book. What if you do it and it sucks?"

"If it sucks, you can burn it, Travis. Just let me try. I think it is the best option for you. Richie agrees. Truth be told, this was his idea."

"Your fiancé knows about this? I talked to him on the phone, and you didn't tell me about y'all's big plan for me?"

"I just did. Travis, I told him that before I could marry him, I needed to help you somehow, that you needed my help and I had to do something. We brainstormed about it, he came up with the perfect idea of me writing your book, and that is why I flew back to Houston. Richie is a great guy. You said so yourself an hour ago."

"I've never met the asshole in person."

They both laughed.

"I don't want to do this, Ava."

"I know," she answered. "But you should. Your daughters deserve it. I will write it the way you would want it written. I know you, and I love you." She leaned back again. "Trust me and my instincts. Bet your life on my instincts. Remember that one?"

Travis shook his head, still in a little shock by what had just occurred. But Ava was right. His daughters had been hurting for years. They were bearing the brunt for his sins, and he wanted them in his life again. Desperately. Maybe it was time, and he couldn't think of another way to have this done. Perhaps this was his best chance.

"Ok," Travis said reluctantly. "But I'll tell it my way."

Chapter 4

T-Mac's

"A froufrou restaurant?" Ava asked, parking her car. "It's 10:00 am, and it looks closed. '*T-Mac's Old Italian Bistro*'? Why here? It looks closed."

"It is closed," Travis said, getting out of the car. "That is why it's perfect. No one will bother us." He grabbed his clubs out of her trunk. "Relax, little girl. Get ready for a big surprise."

They walked through the front doors, instantly greeted with the smells of fresh paint, wood varnish, and Clorox bleach.

"Where the hell have you been?" a voice yelled from across the room.

"I ran into an old buddy," Travis yelled back.

"Oh my God, Uncle Mac, is that you?" Ava asked, jogging toward him now, then jumping into his arms.

Mac was Travis's best friend when Ava was growing up, and he was always around. Back in the day, Mac owned a small restaurant/corner bar place where Travis sometimes brought Ava for lunch, and Mac let her eat and drink cokes for free. He kept pints of chocolate chip ice cream just for her.

"The one and only," Mac laughed, lifting her in the air with his huge arms. "What, did you think I was dead? Oh man, I'm sorry. I'm so sweaty. It's been a busy morning."

"Shut up, like I care," she said, gently punching him in the shoulder. "You look great. Wow, so now you own a fancy restaurant? It's huge, Mac, and what an amazing location. River Oaks. All your customers are rich. What's on the second floor?"

"A brothel," Travis answered, smirking. "We need to talk all afternoon, Mac, and maybe some tonight. Can we use one of the booths in the back?"

"No problem," Mac said. "What are y'all drinking?"

"Jack and Sprite Zero, and waters also. Thank you, Mac."

Ava gave Mac another hug, then followed Travis to a large, half-moon shaped corner booth, sliding in, then plugging a microphone into her laptop and turning on the computer.

"You drink now?" Ava asked.

"Yeah, it loosens the swing," Travis said, looking at her equipment. "What's all that?"

"I'm going to record you," Ava said, placing the mic in-between them, "so you can just let it all out, in your own words." She turned to survey the beautiful main floor of the restaurant again, amazed at the artwork and furniture. "How can he pay for all this?"

"Mac is just a restaurant genius," Travis said. "The restaurant business is tricky, really trendy in this uptown district. Everybody wants to go to the new hotspot in town, so every year or so, Mac gets new furniture and changes the theme. He has a buddy that owns a commercial furniture place, Michael at Lyndsey Furniture, and Mac leases all this stuff from him, so he owns nothing and can change the theme whenever he wants. When Mac wants to change the place, he calls Michael and they take the old and bring new stuff, whatever Mac needs. The complete turnaround, furniture, paint and everything, is about a week. People think it's a new place, even though it has the same basic name, so they flock to it, for a year, then Mac changes everything again. He makes a killing. It was '*T-Mac's Tex-Mex Hacienda*' for the past year, but now it's going to be the ritzy '*T-Mac's Old Italian Bistro*.' His prices are insane, but the idiots keep lining up, trying to be trendy. The guy is a genius."

"Is his name T-Mac now?"

"Nah. It's just the restaurant name. If it works, it works. Now," Travis said, regrouping, "let's talk about this possible book. We need to set some ground rules."

"Ok."

"I tell my story, how I want it. You listen, then type it all down. Right?"

"No. You tell your story, and I'll listen, yes. But when I need something explained, I'll ask you questions, and you will help me understand it better. To do this correctly, I need to understand all the details. We want no one going up to Charlotte or Shelby and asking them questions ever again."

"What if I don't want to give you some of those details?"

"Trust me, Travis."

"Everything ok?" Mac asked, passing out the drinks off a tray, noticing the microphone then glancing at Travis.

"Yeah, it's fine. Thank you, Mac. Can you believe how great Ava looks? She's engaged to a doctor. A surgeon."

"Damn, let another one slip away," Mac said, shaking his head and walking away. "Oh well. Maybe she'll get divorced quick, and I'll have another shot."

"Maybe," Travis laughed, then turned to Ava, letting out a sigh. "Ok. Hell, why not?" He closed his eyes, thought for a few seconds, then opened them again. "Tell me when to start."

Ava grabbed her water but slid the Jack and Sprite Zero toward Travis.

"Oh my God, you're pregnant?"

"No, I'm not pregnant! I just don't drink hard liquor at 10:00 am, Travis. And I can't believe you do now."

"One day," Travis laughed, then took a big swig of her mixed drink, "you are going to be a great mother-in-law."

Chapter 5

The Beginning

Ava pressed record on her computer, then asked, "So how did you meet your wife?"

"I met her at the bar at Marco's Steakhouse. I was a waiter, and she was there with three guys from her law office."

"You were a waiter at Marco's? You? That's the most exclusive restaurant in Houston. How old were you?"

"I was 23, and she was 32. I had worked at Marco's for almost five years. I went to school with Marco's son, Jo-Jo. He played football with me, a wide receiver. Marco loved me, the sports and stuff, so he gave me the job right out of high school."

"Wait," Ava interrupted, "so you never went to college?"

"I got into a few colleges, truthfully everyone that I applied to, but I didn't want to go. It was never something that interested me. After I graduated from high school, I told my parents that I didn't want to go. They threw me out, pretty much disowned me, so I made a life for myself. I went to see Marco, and he gave me a busboy job right on the spot, which saved me. He wanted me to be a waiter, but I needed a lot of training: how to act, how to take an order, how to choose wine and all that stuff, but I took to it pretty quickly. I elevated from a busboy to a waiter in less than a month.

"I liked waitering, and the pay was insane. The prices were extravagant, so I made a fortune, $500+ a night, six nights a week. And the holidays were incredible. I got a $2000 tip once for working a Christmas Eve dinner for twenty. It was incredible for a kid right out of high school. I got to meet politicians, professional athletes, and prominent business people, every night. Marco's was all I cared about until I hit my first golf ball."

"When did you hit your first golf ball?" Ava asked, trying to keep up.

"At 21."

"You had never hit a golf ball until you were 21? You had never played golf at all?"

"Hell no. I played everything but golf. I made fun of golfers. I used to say '*The only thing slower than golf is farming.*' Read it somewhere. It didn't look like a sport to me, but just an elitist pissing contest that only certain people were allowed to play, fixed so only certain people could win. I never would've picked up a golf club if it wasn't for Marco.

"There was a charity scramble, for pancreatic cancer, I think, and Marco paid for a team. One of the players canceled, and he needed a body for the tournament. Marco asked me to join, but I told him that I didn't play. Marco wouldn't take no for an answer, so he had Jo-Jo, his son, take me to a driving range that afternoon. Jo-Jo showed me the basic swing, and I watched some other people swing on the range and figured it out on my own. The golf swing was just a sideways baseball swing, and watching the guys that seemed to know what they were doing, I picked up on two things instantly: how still their heads stayed as the arms and hips rotated, and how the club returned to impact at the same position as it started in the swing. Grabbing a seven iron, I took my first swing, hit the ball, and I fell in love with the game of golf."

"How did it come so easy for you?" Ava asked.

"It felt natural from the first swing. I truly think that I was born to hit a golf ball. Not at birth, but all my training in sports prior to hitting a golf ball prepared me to play golf at a high level instantly. By playing baseball, I understood the golf swing motion. By playing soccer, I understood the spins of a golf ball for chipping and how hitting down on a ball affects the golf ball's flight. By playing basketball, I understood how form and finesse could complement each other. Honestly, golf always felt like I was cheating, like I had a piece of knowledge that others didn't have, couldn't understand or didn't have the patience to learn.

"So learning golf was different for me than others. See, others would go to the range to improve, but I went to the range to hone my craft. Golf seemed like a mystery to other people, but for me, golf was the answer to why I exist and what I was supposed to do in life. It was the purpose that I had always looked for, that I knew was out there, but I hadn't found yet. Golf made me make sense. Do you understand?"

"I think so," Ava answered. "You played in golf tournaments back then, right? How'd you do in them?"

"Just two, both as an amateur and they were on a little mini-tour. I got tenth in the first tournament and learned a lot. I had never really seen or been to a golf tournament before, so it was a little bit of a culture shock. But I figured it all out and won the next tournament by eight strokes."

"You won your second golf tournament? How old were you?"

"Twenty-two. I'd been playing for a year and a half."

"Travis, you are amazing. Why didn't you go pro right then? You could've gotten a sponsor, right?"

"I didn't want a sponsor. I'd only get like 30% if I won. They would get 70%! What a bunch of bull. So I decided to save up my own money to pay for a tour myself. I was going to do it my way and not owe anybody anything. My earnings on the mini-tours would help me make it on the PGA Tour, and if I couldn't earn enough on the mini-tours, I didn't deserve to be on the PGA Tour anyway."

"You are so stubborn," Ava laughed. "You have to do everything your way." She stared at him lovingly, shaking her head. "Were you good at other sports?"

"I was always a pretty good athlete as a kid. It was all that I ever wanted to be, from the first time my father threw a ball at me. In a ball, I saw a world. What I mean is, I found meaning in it all: the practice, the struggle, the goals, and then figuring out how to win. Sports trumped life in every way. Sports were fair, they don't care who your father was or what color you were, and the rules were all laid out for everyone.

"But sports were frowned upon in my family. I came from edu-cators, doctors, and lawyers. Sports were called '*useless folly.*' My grandfather, a history professor, said the only exercise he ever got was going to his jogging friend's funerals. His son, my father, became a lawyer because my grandfather always wanted to be a lawyer, so his son had to become a lawyer. I was to become a lawyer also, but it wasn't for me.

"Anyway, I had the two worst things that could happen to an athlete as a kid: I was small for my age and had a brain, so no one thought sports were a smart path for me. I studied hard because the better my grades were, the more I was allowed to play sports. Then, suddenly, in my junior year of high school, I grew. Six inches that year. By my senior year, I was six feet tall and a force to be reckoned with on any ball field: the quarterback in football, shooting guard in basketball, clean-up batter in baseball, forward in soccer, you name it. I even had a couple of sport scholarship offers. But my father wanted me to go to Stanford, then Stanford Law. It was his dream, and I was supposed to live it for him. My family's dream for me was my nightmare, and they didn't care what I thought. So after high school, I quit their dream, left their lives and moved on.

"Do you miss them?" Ava asked.

"Not a bit. They're Democrats."

"Understood," she laughed, shaking her head at his stubborn-ness. She glanced down at her notes, trying to fill in a gap. "So how did you meet your wife?"

"I was working as a waiter, and there was a woman at the bar with three guys, all of them in business attire. They were lawyers, celebrating a big settlement in a case. Picking up an order at the bar, I heard the woman talking, telling the three guys that she would buy the next round if they could tell her the name of the poet who wrote this, then she recited a few lines from a poem on children's suffrage. They had no idea. I heard her and realized who it was instantly.

"Elizabeth Barrett," I answered, balancing my drinks on a tray.

She turned, completely stunned.

"Yes. You're right. Elizabeth Barrett Browning."

"No, Elizabeth Barrett," I corrected her, walking away. "She wrote it before she married Robert Browning."

"Well, she was blown away. The rest of the evening, she stayed by the wait-station at the bar, even after the three other lawyers left, flirting with me every time I came by to pick up a drink order, pressing me for my name and trying to find out who I was."

"How did you know the poem?" Ava asked.

"Benefits of a classical education," he answered sarcastically, taking a swig of bourbon.

"Were you attracted to her?"

"She was an attractive woman. Very smart, and determined. Long legs. You'd have to be dead not to notice her."

"So you were hot for her also?"

"I was amazed that a woman like that would pay attention to a guy like me. I guess I was flattered, but it wasn't love at first sight or anything." He thought for a second, and then it came to him. "I cared more about golf than her."

"Her name was Lexi, right?"

"Yes, Lexi Bingham. She said that she had the day off tomorrow and would love to see me again. I decided why not? I told her that I tee off at 8:00 am at Memorial Park and she could ride in a cart with me. Lexi thought I was kidding at first, but then she realized I was serious. She said ok, asked what time I would be there, and said she would meet me there at 7:00 am.

"Son of a gun, if she didn't show, had to be hung over, but she hid it well and looked gorgeous." He smiled, feeling it all come back to him after being buried in the back of his mind for so long. "That was a fun day. You see, by that time, I had become a little bit of a golf celebrity."

"Wait," Ava asked, "you were 23, right? You'd only been playing golf for two years. How were you a celebrity? Has it always been like this for you and golf?"

"I was a Memorial Park, muni-guy, golf celebrity. See, after that scramble, I became a golf nut. My hours were perfect to train, so I practiced and played golf all day, every day, mostly at Memorial

Park, then worked as a waiter at night. I got pretty good at golf fast. People loved how I could break par and didn't even know all the rules, and because I was always a single on the walk-on list, I would play with three new people every day, so I got to know all the regulars after only six months. The muni-golfers felt like my mentors, answering all my questions about golf rules and etiquette, showing me how to become a man on a golf course. People took ownership in me and my game, like a coach or a father, and I let them feel that way, listening to them, always thanking them for the knowledge, respecting the history that is Memorial Park, learning about former greats, and trying to follow in their footsteps. Plus, as you know, golfers gravitate toward me."

"Why is that, Travis?"

Travis leaned back, a little uncomfortable.

"It's because I'm not a real golfer." Travis leaned forward again, arranging his thoughts. "Think about it. Think of all the great golfers you've known in life. Aren't most of them jerks? Aren't most of them narcissists? I'd say 99% of the best golfers that I've met are not the greatest human beings that have ever existed. But the game attracts those types. You have to be so egocentric to play golf, almost a narcissist, because of the hours practicing alone and everything. A player naturally becomes aloof over time. Plus, good players hate to play with average players for some reason. They look down on twenty handicappers like Catholics looks down on Protestants, or a rich guy looks down on a poor one.

"I love playing with average golfers, and I hate playing with the jerks. I love making sure someone has a good round and a good time, truthfully more than I care about my own round. If I can play with people and without them knowing, help them play the best game of their life by keeping them relaxed and under control, I feel great. To me, that's golf. So people like playing with me, they usually have a better time on a golf course when they do, and they also enjoy watching me hit a ball, in a way most just can't. They all feel like my friend, because they are, and they become protective of me. I think that is why I'm treated well to this day. Because I care about them as much as I care about my golf, and that isn't normal for a golfer, especially with a better player. That is why I don't think I'm a real golfer."

"That's what you did for me," Ava said, realizing his genius for the first time. "Why? I wasn't a great golfer with potential. Why even waste your time on someone like me?"

"You were a lost little girl with a mixed-up family life. You needed stability and a place to escape from your tough home situation. I taught you how to create stability in your own life by using a golf course, and I helped you escape, by hanging out with me. And you ended up becoming a damn fine golfer. Just because you can't play on the LPGA Tour doesn't make you a waste of my time. The truth is I learned more from you than you did from me."

"Thank you," Ava said. "Thank you for saving my childhood." She wanted to talk to him more about their relationship, flood him with her unanswered questions of her youth and her precious memories, but this was not the time. Reluctantly, she checked her notes again. "Tell me about that first day with Lexi."

"It was perfect. When Lexi arrived, a maintenance guy picked her up in a golf cart and drove her to me at the range. I told him to look out for her. While she watched me warm-up, people came by to say '*Hi*' and I would introduce them to Lexi. They were accountants, roofers, bankers, politicians, carpenters, lawyers, people from all walks of life."

"You know everybody," Lexi whispered, blown away.

"We got in the cart, and I drove to the putting green. After I finished my putting warm-up, I sat in the cart next to Lexi, who gently grabbed my hand in her excitement over everything. I explained to her that I teed off at 8:00 am every morning, and I never knew whom I was going to play with each day. This morning, it was pretty hilarious because about a dozen golfers were arguing with the starter, trying to get in my group. I think they wanted to look at Lexi for eighteen holes. So we teed off, I hit last, and I pounded one, right down the left-center. People clapped and cheered from the adjacent putting green, '*Go Travis!*,' '*Boom Shacka-Lacka*,' like they always did back in those days. Lexi, startled at first, started clapping and laughing at all the commotion also.

"I played great that day. We all did. Lexi knew very little about golf, but even she could tell that something special was going on. She had a blast, joking around with the other golfers, and listening to their golf stories about me, and they loved looking at her. After the round, we went to lunch, and all she could talk about was the golf course, calling me famous and all that stuff. That lunch went on for three hours. I walked her to her car, then she suddenly turned and kissed me. It was a great kiss."

"I went to work that night, wondering if she would show, but she never came by Marco's. After my shift, I walked outside and there she was, parked right out front. '*Get in, Slugger*' was all she said. Lexi drove me to her house, and by the next morning, I was hers."

Chapter 6

Dreams and Change

"Life instantly changed."

"How so?" Ava asked.

"Lexi became my whole life. I'd cut out of golf early and lunch with her during the week, and she'd hang out at Marco's bar while I worked at night, working on her laptop all night waiting for me to get off, then we crashed at her place. After a month, I got rid of my apartment and moved in with her. She never complained about my golf, and I understood about her busy work schedule. It was perfect.

"After two months, she started to get serious."

"Travis, what are your dreams in life?" Lexi asked one Sunday morning, lying in bed.

"I'd like to try professional golf. I've saved $87,000, and when I get to $100,000, I can afford a full year playing on a mini-tour. I just want to find out if I'm good enough. If I am, I'll start living the dream. If I find out that I can't, that's ok also. I just want to know if I have what it takes."

"What about kids?"

"Kids aren't an option for me. I don't have a college degree, and I couldn't support them in the manner that I should. It would be cruel for a man like me, who chose the path that I did, to have children."

Lexi started to cry.

"I can't have children. I had cervical cancer in my early twenties and had to go through chemo. It left me unable."

"I'm so sorry."

"It's ok," Lexi said, trying to smile. "I just never thought that I would find a man who would not need children that I could love. I guess God does work in mysterious ways. And I love you, Travis. I could love you forever."

Then I said, "I love you, too."

"We took the red-eye to Las Vegas that night and got married."

"You married Lexi after just two months?"

"I know. I married my wife and I had never seen her office and never met one of her friends. Hell, I knew almost nothing about her at all. Pretty crazy, huh?"

"Oh, Travis," Ava said, floored.

"I was in love. We flew home the next morning from Vegas, never had a honeymoon. I needed to practice golf, and she had some big cases going on. Lexi helped set up a new bank account for me and filled it with a little more money to make it equal $100,000. My dream was fulfilled. I quit my job and began trying to figure out which mini-tour to play the next year. Then it happened."

"A month into marriage, I drove home from golf practice, and Lexi's car was in the driveway. She never beat me home. I opened the front door, and she ran to hug me, jumping up and down."

"I'm pregnant," Lexi said, handing me a home pregnancy stick-thingy.

"You're what?"

"I'm pregnant. I took three tests, and they all were positive. It's a miracle."

"She told me that she had been feeling bad when she woke up for the past week and wondered if it was morning sickness. Lexi was so happy that I couldn't do anything but say it was great. Two days later, we went to see her gynecologist. Lexi gave a urine sample, and the pregnancy was confirmed. She was three months pregnant."

"Three months?" Ava gasped.

"Yeah," Travis said, taking a big swig from his drink. "So I asked the doctor how rare it was for an ex-cancer patient to get pregnant, and if there any complications we should prepare ourselves for in the future. The gynecologist gave me this crazy look and asked why I would propose such a question."

"Because my wife had cervical cancer and went through chemo in her early twenties," I said.

"Lexi started laughing, saying that I was just stressed and didn't know what I was saying. The doctor tried to smile then shook his head as he left the room. Right when the door closed, Lexi slapped my face. Hard."

"Don't you ever do something like that again!" she yelled, her eyes glaring right through me. "From now on, I ask the questions, not you. Let the adults talk, and you just sit there looking pretty."

"Obviously, I realized that I had just made the biggest mistake of my life. We had taken separate cars, so I hustled out of the office and drove like mad to our bank, to get my money out of the new account, but she closed the account weeks ago. She had set up new accounts that needed Lexi's approval in order for me to access any money. My money was under her control, I had no job and no place to live. Worse, I was too embarrassed to tell anybody what had just happened. I was trapped."

"So I got home and she greeted me, lovingly, like nothing had happened, asking me about baby names or some such thing. I asked her about the bank accounts, and she said she had to change them, in case I ran out on her now that she was pregnant, that men do that a lot. She explained that golf didn't matter now because my golf playing was over.

"You're a father now," Lexi explained. "You're not a child anymore. Now you are here for us, our child and me. Your job is just to take care of us now. A stay-at-home-dad. This child is the greatest thing that has ever happened to you, and you don't even realize it yet. I did this for you. I'm making you the man that you were meant to be. In a few years, you'll be thanking me. You'll no longer be a joke. You're my husband now, and you're important."

"The next day I went to see the only guy that I trusted in the world. Mac." Travis raised his hand, signaling for another round of drinks. Mac gave him a thumbs-up.

"How did you know Mac?" Ava asked.

"He was the night manager at Marcos, a former cook, and my boss when I worked there. He was a smart guy who I always trusted, and I loved working for Mac those five years. I told him my situation, and he gave me some tough advice. He said that I was a golfer, and golfers always play it as it lies. So I needed to suck it up and make the best of all this. Not for me, but for my child. I had put my child in this situation, and I needed to protect my child. He explained that it was lucky that I got to stay home with the child because I could protect the child from Lexi, that my child needed protection. He told me to go home, prepare for the child, and make it the best marriage that it can be. When the child left home, I could leave. So that's what I did."

"That's insane," Ava countered.

"No, little girl. That's life. And life isn't fair."

"Life's not fair, blah-blah-blah," Mac said mockingly, reloading the drinks and grabbing the old ones. "I'm marrying a doctor, and I'm a great golfer, but life's not fair. I'm drunk at noon on a weekday cuz life's not fair. Boo-hoo-hoo."

"Shut up, Mac, you old bastard," Travis laughed, then toasted him for the reload.

"So I sucked it up, put down the golf clubs and started preparing for a child, doing all the Lamaze and baby classes with Lexi, reading anything that I could get my hands on concerning babies and child care, and trying to create a life with my new wife. Then she goes into labor a couple of weeks early. We head to the hospital, and thirteen hours later, out came Charlotte Louise Hatfield. I named her. I always liked Charlotte's Web, and Louise was my cool grandmother's name. The sad part was I named her because Lexi didn't care.

"When the nurses brought the baby into the room, Lexi told them to let me hold her. Man, Charlotte was a cutie, and so small. I could hold her in one hand. That moment blew me away. The nurses left, and I asked Lexi again if she wanted to hold her."

"You don't even care that we had a girl, do you?" she asked, caustically. "You are such a pussy. What kind of man doesn't want a son? Truth is you're probably not man enough to have a son. So instead, we have a girl. Just what the world needs, another whore in the world."

"Then Lexi rolled over and fell asleep," Travis said, taking a big sip from his Jack and Sprite Zero.

Chapter 7

———◆———

A Better Understanding

Ava stood up, walked around for a few seconds, then sat back down again.

"Wait, Travis. You're skipping over way too much."

"How so?"

"I mean, Lexi was the greatest thing ever, and then she's calling her first born child a whore?"

"Pretty much. That's the way it happened."

"But how, Travis? Who was she? I mean, what type of lawyer was she, and what type of person was she? She makes no sense to me."

"Well," Travis said, "Lexi never really made sense. She was a manipulator. A fake, or an imposter. She used people to achieve her goals in life. She was a corporate lawyer, stuff like contract and securities law, I think. I never really cared. I know she wasn't very good at it, but that didn't matter to her. She moved up the ladder by using people, manipulating and trapping them. Her goal in life was to be powerful but not work very hard. She wanted to be feared, and she loved controlling other people's lives."

"How did you not see this in her?"

"She was a pro at it when I met her, and I was young and stupid. I discovered right before Lexi died that she was married twice before, so I wasn't her first sucker. The first guy paid for her college and law school. The second guy helped her make partner at her law firm."

"Oh my God, Travis. She was married twice before, and you married her?"

"I had no idea that she was twice divorced. Both divorces claimed spousal abuse, and it was probably true. Lexi could do things to make a man want to hit her. She got a lot of money from both guys in the divorces. She'd find your button and just keep pressing, laughing at you the whole time."

"Did you ever hit her?" Ava asked.

"No. I did everything that I could to protect my children. I just sat back and took it. No way I would let her win. You know me, I'm a stubborn ass."

"What did Lexi want from you?"

"A child. I guess that old biological clock was going off inside her and she was looking for a donor. I met her criteria, knowing the answer to her silly poem question. Elizabeth Barrett. Can you believe it? So she got her kid. But I put a wrinkle on her little plan. I wouldn't leave. No matter what she did, I wouldn't leave. I had to protect Charlotte from my mistake."

"What was Lexi like to live with?"

"Horrid," Travis smirked, taking a quick sip of Jack. "After we got married, each day was worse. I think she was one of those people that just liked the chase in relationships. Once she got you, she hated you, and just wanted to torture you with cutting words and acts of shaming you. At first, it was subtle, but over time, they became more overt and obviously intentional, trying to make me leave."

"Like what, Travis?"

"Well, before we got married, it was all perfume and lingerie, but after saying '*I do*,' all Lexi wore to bed were warm-up pants and sweatshirts. Then, right before the baby was born, she turned one of the guest bedrooms into my bedroom. Lexi kicked me out of the bed that she used to seduce and trick me into marrying her. She said that when the baby was born, the child would sleep with her and I needed to go to a different room. She explained that it was unfair that I got to spend all day with our child and she had to work because I had no job and was worthless. It would only be fair for her to spend her nights with the baby.

"I just said ok, for two big reasons. One, I hated sleeping in the same bed with Lexi. She was such a phony and a liar, I hated being in the same room with her, much less laying next to her. I was ecstatic to be out of that bed. And two, I knew she wouldn't sleep with the baby in her room for long. After two nights, she put the crib in my bedroom, explaining that she worked for a living and needed her sleep. I knew she could not take care of a baby. She hated anything that was demanding and needed constant attention. I don't think she could take care of a cat, much less an infant.

"So without doing anything, I had gotten Charlotte and myself out of her bedroom. That was a good day." Travis snickered to himself, remembering. "Pretty pathetic. But that's what living with Lexi was like."

"I just don't get it, Travis. How could you have another child with this monster?"

Travis downed the rest his Jack and Sprite Zero, then pulled the other one toward him. He thought for a second, then just said it.

"I didn't."

"What?" Ava asked, floored.

"Ava, I have blonde hair. Lexi had blonde hair. Charlotte has blonde hair. But Shelby has black curly hair."

"What are you saying, Travis?"

"Lexi was having trouble at work. I think her ineptness was showing with a new client, and she couldn't figure out how to fix things. She became erratic, a nightmare. I don't know how she acted at work, but at home, she was a terror, really drinking heavily and screaming a lot. But then things got better, a few months after Charlotte's first birthday. I remember Lexi being almost tolerable, like her life had gotten better or something. I had no idea. A few months later, I noticed her clothes being a little tight around the belly, then it became obvious. She was pregnant."

"So you had another kid with her?"

"I hadn't slept with Lexi since the scene at the gynecologist's office, almost two years before. After all the lies and living with the psycho, I didn't want to touch Lexi ever again. And she had no interest in me anymore. It couldn't have been me."

Ava asked, "Who?"

"Her boss. She figured out a way to keep her job."

Ava thought to herself and realized how obvious it was that Shelby wasn't Travis's biological daughter. As a little girl, Ava never thought about it or questioned it. But now, it made perfect sense.

"You raised another man's child?"

"I confronted Lexi," Travis continued. "She confessed, of course, because it was obvious. Lexi said that she had complete job security now, that she had done it for Charlotte, and me. And she said that I could raise this child, just like Charlotte."

"How did you not leave her, Travis?"

"I almost did, but it made life better. You see, now I knew a big secret that could destroy her life. Lexi needed me, so I got treated better. Not like a husband, but like a beneficial worker. She treated me with more respect, and she knew that I was an important piece to her puzzle of a life. So Charlotte's life would be better also."

"Travis, that is insane!"

"Yes, it is," he said, taking a sip. "But that was my life. If I tried to divorce her, I'd never see Charlotte again, and no telling who would raise her. So my whole life was protecting Charlotte. Plus, once Shelby was born, I had to take care of her. She was so precious and had nobody. She became my daughter from the first moment that I laid eyes on her. Shelby is and always will be my daughter."

Travis put his head down.

"I was looking at Shelby through the window of the maternity ward, a couple of hours after she was born," Travis began, like it hurt to say each word. "I was holding Charlotte and just looking through the glass at Shelby, realizing how my life had changed and thinking about all that I had in front of me for the next 18 years. Then I heard a voice say, '*You better take real good care of my little girl, boy, or, I swear, I'll kill you.*' Charlotte squirmed a little on my shoulder, so it took me a second to turn around. When I did, I saw a man in a black suit walking toward the elevators with his back to me. He had black curly hair." Travis let out a big sigh. "He died when Shelby was a sophomore in high school, and as far as I know, he never bothered her. It was the only time that I ever saw him."

Chapter 8

———◆———

The Learning

Travis headed toward the men's room. After pausing the recorder on her computer, Ava stretched, then walked over toward Mac, who was putting some finishing touches on the bar area.

"When did Travis start drinking?"

"When the girls left," Mac answered, wiping down a glass shelf. "What, a man can't have a drink anymore?"

"I'm just worried about him. He seemed like the same guy on the golf course, but I don't remember him like this. Travis seems—. He seems tired. Too tired."

"He's just older now, Ava, and so are you. Travis is the same guy, just different priorities now. What are you guys doing anyway?"

"She's trying to help Charlotte and Shelby," Travis said, motioning Ava back toward the table. "Refills, Mac, if you please."

"In a bit. I ordered a couple of pizzas. Should be here any minute. I'll refill when it arrives."

"You're the best, Mac," Travis yelled, sitting back down.

"I'm going to be a blimp for a bride," Ava said, sliding back into the booth and pressing record. "Whataburger for breakfast and pizza for lunch. What do you eat for dinner?"

"Ice cream. Where were we?"

"Shelby was born," Ava said, looking at her notes.

"Ah, yes, the life of a stay-at-home dad," Travis began. "That's what we should write a book about."

"Really. Why, Travis?"

"Because people need to understand what it is like for a guy to raise children from infancy. No one gets it. See, being a stay-at-home dad is hard, but not because guys can't do it or suck at it. It just goes against nature. Dads are different from moms.

"Dads are problem solvers. If we hear a child cry, we try to figure out what the crying means: is the child hungry? is she hurt? does she need a diaper? whatever. A mom hears a child cry, and she just runs and hugs the child. So a guy naturally makes taking care of a kid more difficult on himself, more of an effort, where a mom just comforts the kid and deals with the reason in her own sweet time.

"Dads aren't made to take care of infants. If a dad gets lost in the woods with a baby, the baby dies. If a mom gets lost with a baby, the baby has food. And I promise you, the baby knows it. My children would take a bottle from me, but they knew that Lexi had the fresh milk. You could tell in their eyes that I was not the total package when it came to their nourishment. But once they were old enough for solid food, they were like, 'Hey, you're not so bad. *You do serve a purpose.*' Lexi nursed the girls for 18 months each, so they bonded food-wise with her."

"Wow," Ava said, "so Lexi was a good mom when the girls were young?"

"No. Lexi did nurse the kids in the evening sometimes, and pumped milk for my bottles at work during the day, but she loved how big her boobs got when the kids were born. She'd wear these short sleeveless blouses and push-up bras, really looked like a tramp, which she was. I'm sure she loved the attention. Whatever. I just needed the bottles. When the girls stopped nursing, she got a boob job to keep up the facade. It was so obvious, but she got a huge bonus that year, so they worked. I guess you could say that they paid for themselves real quick."

"What was your relationship like with Lexi?"

"Um, I was like a nanny. She wanted no part of taking care of the kids, so I raised them on my own. I'd see her when she got home at night, like 8:30 pm after she ate dinner somewhere, but she left for work like 5:30 am, or wherever she went when she left. I had no idea and didn't care."

"Did y'all kiss goodnight or talk at all?"

"No. We'd say hello or whatever, but that was about it."

"Did she spend time with the girls?"

"Sometimes on the weekends. We'd go to a movie or something. Sometimes to a mall. But we never really did anything in public together, and Lexi didn't want to take care of the girls alone. A couple of times a year she would take the girls on a weekend trip to Galveston, without me, to the Ambassador Resort and Spa. They had a nanny service at the resort, so Lexi didn't have to do anything. She didn't want anyone to see her with a husband, I guessed. See, Lexi never wore a wedding ring and never wanted to appear to have a family in her business life. She wanted others to think of her as a woman who didn't need a man, as independent, as available. Sex was a weapon for her, a tool to trap a guy or get out of trouble."

"Pizza, pizza," Mac said, laying two boxes on the table. "Pepperoni and green peppers for him, and hamburger and onion for her."

"How could you remember?" Ava asked, looking at her favorite pizza as a kid.

"I'm a food guy," Mac said, pleased with himself, reloading the table with drinks again. "Here are some paper towels. Enjoy."

"You da' man!" Travis said, loving his drink and opening the pizza box.

"You never went to her law office?" Ava asked, in between bites.

"Nope. I was never invited, not even the girls, but I never really cared. Some of her co-workers did attend her funeral. Most said they never knew she was married. Her personal secretary came up to me after the service and said I should know that Lexi had cheated on me, more than once. I pretended to care, thanked her profusely for telling me, then left with the girls as soon as possible.

"There is so much that I still don't even know about Lexi. It was an unbelievable situation to have been in, and it almost seems like a dream now. Or a nightmare, sometimes."

"How did you do it, Travis? How did you not break?"

"I was focused. I knew my objective, and I just did my duty. Also, you got to remember, I was married for only six years, who knows if I could've made it twenty years. Probably not, but we'll never know."

"Only six years," Ava repeated, shaking her head. She might have to re-think this marriage stuff. "So tell me more about being a stay-at-home dad."

"I met an eighty-year-old woman right before Charlotte was born, met her in a line at the grocery store of all things, and she told me two important things about being a stay-at-home dad.

"One, she said that the reason men don't stay at home with the kids is that it's harder than going to work every day. And she was right. You are on 24/7, and you can't relax. If you do, even for a moment, something terrible could happen, and you would never forgive yourself. You never realize how much you goof-off at work until you take care of a kid. When you are in charge of a young child, it is constant stress, paying attention and plotting your next move. Hell, just finding thirty seconds to go to the bathroom is an undertaking.

"And two, the couple has to understand that a woman's need to have a kid is equal to a man's need to set and achieve goals. If the husband resents his wife's yearning for children, it will never work. He will do a lousy job. Or, if the wife does not allow the husband to set and achieve goals on the side, some part-time job or hobby, she will destroy him. She has to understand her husband's needs are just as critical as hers. Otherwise, both will fail.

"That was some of the best advice that I got from anyone. It all held true over time. The job was harder than I realized, and my brain started to get fried because Lexi never allowed me to have a hobby or job, like golf.

"Why?" Ava begged. "She saw you play golf and knew how gifted you were. Why was golf off-limits?"

"Control," Travis began, grabbing another slice of his pizza. "She liked having me completely dependent on her. I had to give up golf to be with her because, without golf, I had nothing in life in her eyes and would never leave. It was her way of breaking me and showing that she had complete control over me. Also, she couldn't take credit for my golf. She was the only one in the relationship who was allowed to do well, and my golf threatened her little world. Plus, I think she felt like she was protecting me, in some weird way."

"Didn't you miss golf?"

"I didn't think about it. I had a job to do."

"Come on, Travis," Ava scoffed.

"Ok, yeah," Travis admitted, "I missed it. I missed it a lot." Travis took a big sip from his drink. "The thing that I remember the most was the wind. Whether it was blowing through a tree outside the kitchen window, or running through my hair when I played outside with the girls, it felt like time slipping away, like my golf window was closing. I hated the wind. I just wanted a chance. A chance to find out if I was any good at competitive golf, and I felt my time slipping away, disappearing like the wind."

Chapter 9

―◆―

A New World

"What was Charlotte like as a baby?" Ava asked.

"Like any first child. The most beautiful and precious thing that I'd ever seen, but a scary mystery to take care of on my own. I was entirely out of my element, and as a guy, I didn't want to read any directions or anything. I worked by trial and error: what temperature should the bath be, how often do you feed her, how do you get her to sleep, all that stuff, which may sound like nothing to you right now, but these are some of the most complicated problems that you'll ever have in life. You'll see one day.

"But Charlotte was amazing. She almost seemed patient with me. After six months, we learned how to work together. I figured out her feeding schedule, I took her to the park every day so she could swing; we'd go to the zoo so she could make animal noises, all that stuff. I taught her how to walk really early, at eight months, which was stupid."

"Why was that stupid?" Ava asked, enjoying a side of Travis that she had never known.

"I had to watch her more closely now because she could fall. Dumbest thing that I ever did in life. Charlotte wasn't steady until 11 months, so for three months, I had to be right next to her at all times. But it was fun holding her hands and showing her the world on her own two feet."

"When did Charlotte start talking?"

"At about 18 months. A little late, but Charlotte became great at it. 18 months was an important age as a parent because she finally could communicate with me, ask me for what she really wanted, like milk or apple juice or water, which is a lot easier than guessing. Also, if she felt sick, Charlotte could finally say if her tummy or ears or throat hurt, which, again, was a lot easier than guessing. But even better, I could explain to her that the medicine would make her feel better and that the pain would go away, so she knew that I was trying to make things better. I could finally tell her that I loved her and the medicine would help her pain, and she could understand me."

"Did Lexi go to the doctor with y'all?" Ava asked.

"No," Travis laughed. "If the baby even sniffled, she would run away. *'I'm the breadwinner, and I can't get sick. Keep that disease ball away from me.'* When Lexi was on the warpath, I would tell her that the girls were sick and she should stay away from them. It worked great, like a wooden stake to a vampire."

"Then Shelby was born. I worried for Charlotte because we had spent so much time together, I thought maybe she would think that I had abandoned her for Shelby, but Charlotte's reaction was the complete opposite. She loved her new baby sister and liked having more time to herself. She was a protective and loving big sister."

"No terrible two's?" Ava asked surprised.

"No way, either girl. Terrible two's is a myth. The children that have problems at that age are children who need more attention. If your child is a terror at two, it's the parents' fault, unless the kid is evil or something.

"My favorite age was three years old. At three, they start to understand why you taught them their ABC's. They start to wonder how a car works, what stars are for, why dogs all look different, and they love how you have all the answers. At three, they understand that they're not the center of the universe, and you help them understand that being a part of a whole is not only ok, but the way life works, and they start to feel more a part of things. They learn that they are a part of a family, a country, and a world. It's pretty cool."

"You liked taking care of them," Ava said.

"Yeah, I guess. It was so much more than I thought it was going to be. But it was lonely."

"How so?"

"As a guy, you don't have an outlet of any kind. See, women have play dates and different things that they do together with young kids. They put the kids in a giant pen in the middle of the living room with some toys, while they drink wine and gossip. They go to the mall together and shop with the kids. They go to the country club and swim in the kiddie-pool together. But a guy can't do any of that."

"Why not?"

"Can you imagine what Lexi would've said if I hung out with other women all day? Can you imagine what their husbands would've said? Plus, women don't want a guy around."

"How so?"

"Here's an example. I was pushing Charlotte in a stroller through our neighborhood when a Suburban pulled up beside me. A woman leaned out the driver's window, asked how old my child was, and I answered six months. She gushed, saying how they have a Wednesday morning playgroup of infants, that my wife should bring Charlotte by and join them. I explained that I stay home with the baby, and she literally said, '*Oh, well you can't come*,' and she drove off, never to be seen again.

"No way," Ava laughed.

"Swear. It happened all the time. Mothers were cruel to me as a stay-at-home dad, much worse than guys. They constantly tried to point out something that you were doing wrong, and obviously wanted me to fail. I was threatening to women, doing the job that they told their husbands every night that a man could never do. But guys were nice to me, mostly jealous. They barely saw their kids and wished they had more of a relationship with them. They saw me, how my kids loved and respected me, and they were envious. All their kids ever did was ask them for money, and all their wives did was complain that there wasn't enough money or how the house wasn't big enough. Guys were nice, and women were jerks."

"What else would women do?"

"Here's one. Charlotte was three years old and wanted to ride the carousel at the mall, so I brought both girls one morning. Charlotte rode her horse while I held one-year-old Shelby on another one. We rode around a few times, and then Charlotte needed to use the bathroom. You see, Charlotte had just got potty-trained and loved using new bathrooms, especially a big public one, a real pain in the ass but Charlotte loved it. So we go into the men's bathroom, stroller and all, I go into a stall with both kiddos, she does her business, then we head out of the stall. Unexpectedly, four police officers were outside the stall, waiting for us. They grabbed Charlotte, took Shelby right out of my arms, and pushed me against a wall, face-first, then started frisking me. I asked what was going on and they explained that I had made a group of mothers nervous when I entered the men's room with the girls. In order to prove that I wasn't a child molester, I had to show them pictures of my kids from my wallet. This event was before iPhones, so I was lucky to have any photo. The officers questioned me for an hour. As we left, I saw the mothers laughing at us. Charlotte never asked to go to the carousel again.

"Here's another one. We all went to the grocery store one cold morning. We got inside, and I grabbed a shopping cart. I put Charlotte in the main bed of the cart and placed Shelby in the kiddie-seat in the front of the cart. They were all bundled up because it was cold outside, so I started removing their jackets and gloves in the store. Shelby's knit hat fell onto the ground, unbeknownst to me. I started pushing the cart toward the first aisle, when some woman behind me picked up the knit hat, grabbed my arm and started yelling at me, saying that I was a horrible father. She berated me about how important a winter hat was for an infant in cold weather and how reckless I was to have lost it. Just then, a large woman came waddling into the store with an infant under her arm, the infant wearing just a diaper. I pointed her out to my female jerk and said she better yell at that lady now. The female jerk called me an asshole and walked off.

"Another one. A Pastor asked me out to lunch at a Mexican restaurant. I brought fifteen-month-old Shelby and three-year-old Charlotte along also. So we got seated, the waiter grabbed a high chair for Shelby and then brought chips and salsa. I explain to the waiter that my fifteen-month-old was too young for tortilla chips and asked if he could bring some flour tortillas for Shelby to nibble on instead. So the waiter brought the tortillas, I put a napkin on the table, because a plate was too dangerous for a fifteen-month-old, and I tore a tortilla into little pieces for Shelby to nibble on. I had a sippy-cup full of apple juice for Shelby to drink, so she was all set. The Pastor and I started talking, when a few minutes later a woman ran up yelling at us, explaining that an infant cannot eat tortilla chips. I explained to her that Shelby was eating tortilla pieces, not a chip; the woman apologized, then walked away. Five minutes later, another woman does the same thing. The Pastor confronted her this time and acted a little upset at her accusation, saying he was offended by her attitude. I touched his shoulder and said it was all right. I even thanked the woman. She walked away, satisfied. He asked me if this had ever happened before, I explained to him that it happened every day and it was best not to offend them. That was what they wanted."

"That's horrible," Ava said. "Did the women realize how rude they were?"

"Of course. They didn't care, Ava. They felt like they're rescuing the child from Mister Man who knew nothing. It happened all the time. But once the girls got to be five or six, the mothers stopped harassing me. All of a sudden, they loved me. They were lonely, burned-out, and hated their husbands for never paying attention to them or the kids, so when they saw me doting on my children, they started treating me like a superhero. I went from being yelled at to hit on in a matter of years. It was an amazing sociological experiment."

"What were you like at that time?" Ava asked. "You had to be a mess."

"I was fried also. Definitely at my breaking point. My mind was shot, and I was incredibly lonely. Not lonely for a woman, I was sick of them. I was lonely for a purpose, and selfishly, for gratitude. The kids were great, but they were young, needy and demanding. Lexi came home drunk every night, never giving a damn about the kids or me, and constantly explaining to me how much harder her life was than mine, then passing out.

"But something big happened that changed everything for me. It changed my life as a dad and a man.

"One afternoon, when Charlotte was three and Shelby was fifteen months, I put the girls down for their nap and was preparing to do a load of laundry. Trying to be quiet, I snuck upstairs and picked up a few dirty clothes off the floor in Charlotte's room. Suddenly, I heard her voice."

"Thank you, Daddy. I love you."

"I quickly turned. There Charlotte was, sitting up on the side of the bed, smiling, with her arms outstretched, wanting a hug. I had never seen her like this before. I walked over, hugged her long and hard, then gently let her go. Charlotte smiled again, then collapsed back down, rolled over and fell asleep.

"I walked out of her room, fell on my knees and cried. I can't tell you the weight that suddenly lifted off of my shoulders. It's still the most significant moment of my life, hands down. You see, at that moment, I realized that I was not alone. I realized that someone was looking out for me and was proud of me because that was not my daughter talking to me.

"That was God.

"God had used my daughter, a little girl who had never done anything like that before in her life, to thank me for what I was doing, that God respected my efforts, and that God loved me. It was exactly what I needed to hear. I thought no one knew or cared about what I was going through, but God told me that He was proud of me, that I had made the right decision. From that point on, raising my daughters was a blessing and never a chore. That night, I found a church near our house."

"Epiphany Lutheran," Ava said. "You didn't always go to church?"

"No. I had never been to a church. The next day, I met the Pastor, and we had lunch at the Mexican restaurant, that lunch I talked about earlier with the tortillas and the mothers bothering us. The Pastor and I became great friends and still are to this day. The church also had a school, so I enrolled Charlotte in their preschool program, and Shelby started when she was three. My children learned about God at an early age and still are Christians today. I'm very proud of that. And after your father died, when you were seven, I brought you to church and paid for your schooling at Epiphany. I'm very proud that you are still a Christian, Ava.

"After God spoke through my child, I changed my life, became a Christian, and have never been alone again. You see, it was loneliness that was destroying me, a loneliness that I was living a life that was pointless, just spinning my wheels for no reason. A life that no man had ever lived before me because I was just stupid. But the Bible showed me that I was not unique in my marriage, that I placed in this situation for a reason."

"Oh, Travis, I disagree," Ava interrupted. "You had no idea what you were getting yourself into, and she trapped you."

"So?" Travis answered. "Did Moses know what he was getting himself into when he saw the burning bush? Did the disciples know what they were getting themselves into when they started following Jesus? Or, more appropriately, did Adam know what he was getting himself into when he took a bite of Eve's apple? No. But Adam didn't leave Eve after he ate the apple. And Moses still went back to Egypt, knowing he could be charged with the murder of a guard and put to death. And the disciples still spread the word of Christ, knowing their lives would be in danger for as long as they walked the earth. Why? Because it was the right thing to do in life. They did it because it was right and it honored God.

"Do you understand how comforting it was that it honored God that I didn't leave my girls when they needed me most? That I wasn't some sort of idiot for staying with Lexi? That I had served a higher purpose in life by staying and dealing with Lexi, and protecting my children? That I wasn't alone in my situation? Another man would've beaten Lexi, most every man would've abandoned my girls, and few would've blamed the men for their actions. But God knew I could handle the situation, and I thank God that He put me in that position and not someone else who would've struggled.

"My favorite passages from the Bible are:

Ephesians 5:25: 'Husbands, love your wives, just as Christ loved the church and gave himself up for her'

1 Peter 3:7: 'Husbands, in the same way be considerate as you live with your wives, and treat them with respect as the weaker partner and as heirs with you of the gracious gift of life, so that nothing will hinder your prayers.'

Mark 10:9: 'Therefore what God has joined together, let no one separate.'

Proverbs 3:3-4: 'Let love and faithfulness never leave you; bind them around your neck, write them on the tablet of your heart. Then you will win favor and a good name in the sight of God and man.'

Proverbs 31:10: 'A wife of noble character who can find? She is worth far more than rubies.'

Proverbs 30:18-19: "'There are three things that are too amazing for me, four that I do not understand: the way of an eagle in the sky, the way of a snake on a rock, the way of a ship on the high seas, and the way of a man with a young woman.'"

"I can't tell you how great it was to learn in the Bible that I wasn't alone in my struggles, that many guys had struggled before me, and my struggles were minor compared to some of them. My struggles now had meaning and were respected, by no other than Almighty God. I no longer felt alone. I felt like a man with a purpose."

Ready for another round, Travis signaled Mac with an outstretched arm.

"I never realized, Travis," Ava confessed. "I knew you loved God, and you loved me, but I never realized how much God had helped you in life, and how much you needed God. I was just a child who saw a gifted golfer who had it all. I never realized how much you struggled. You hid it well."

"God has a plan for everyone, Ava, but sometimes His plan is hard to understand. The key is not fighting His plan, but trying to recognize it as you go through life. Sometimes you can't see how God is working in your life, especially in hard times, but you realize years later what God was doing. See, God can give you struggles, other times blessings, but at the time He gives them to you, it can be hard to tell the difference between the two. I've found most of my struggles in life have ended up being my greatest blessings, but I definitely didn't recognize it at the time when God gave them to me.

"You were one of my greatest blessings from God, Ava, and I recognized that it was my job to take care of you. You were exactly what I needed on that day, and I was exactly what you needed to help you before you went to college. We were just lucky to let God work in us and that we recognized that we needed each other. We both needed each other, even if we didn't know it at the time."

Smiling, Travis stared at Ava now, fond memories racing through his mind. Then, just as quickly, he became melancholic, glaring into the distance, his mind drifting off into a darker world. Trying to snap himself back, Travis, a little tipsy, stood, looked up and raised his drink high in the air.

"All I know is God has a terrific sense of humor, but a horrible sense of timing," Travis said, laughed to himself, then fell back down into the booth seat. "But I love Him dearly, and I am truly blessed. So I tried to be the best husband that I could from that point on."

"Wait," Ava said. "You found God and decided to become a better husband?"

"Lexi was my wife," Travis said. "God wanted me to treat her like a queen, so I decided to start treating her like a queen."

"You have got to be kidding me."

"No. I got up early the next morning and made Lexi coffee before she left at 5:30 am. I hugged her, thanked her for all she did as a provider for the kids and me, and told her to have a great day."

"Are you crazy?" Ava asked.

"Yes, he is and was," Mac said, reloading the drinks and disposing of the pizza boxes.

"She cheated on you daily," Ava said. "Trapped you. Ruined all your dreams. She didn't even wear a wedding ring. So you woke up early and made her coffee?"

"She's got a point," Mac blurted out as he left.

"Well, yeah. But Lexi was my wife, and I was sick of hating her. I just wanted to be friends. Plus, the Bible said to honor and cherish her, until I die."

"Travis," Ava mumbled, shaking her head. "Well, ok. What did Lexi say?"

"She asked what I wanted, thought I was pulling a con on her or something. After a week, she said I was acting like a pussy and to stop. But I didn't. I made her coffee in the mornings, made her bed every day, and made sure the girls hugged her when she got home.

"On Shelby's fourth birthday, we had a little party at the house. I bought a cake, and Shelby asked Lexi to cut it for us. Lexi cut the cake, then handed Shelby the first piece. Shelby said thank you, and I love you, Mommy. Lexi was startled, then she looked at me.

"We all love you, Lexi," I said. "Thanks for a great birthday for Shelby."

"We sat there eating birthday cake, like a real family, then Shelby asked Lexi when her birthday was. Lexi said she couldn't remember. Then Charlotte asked her also, saying everybody knows what day their birthday was on."

"Ok," Lexi said, still rattled by all this. "My birthday. Um. My birthday is on the 21st, in three weeks. That's my birthday, July 21st."

"So the girls and I planned a big night. On the 21st, we got balloons, streamers, a cake, presents and everything. We waited all evening, but Lexi never showed. I told the girls that she had to work late or something, and put them to bed. I stayed up a little longer, but nothing, so I went to bed also.

"I was falling asleep, then I jumped up, scared out of my mind because I saw someone next to my bed. It was Lexi, and it was 3:00 am. She had black tearstains on her cheeks and stunk of brandy. I told her Happy Birthday and asked if she was ok."

"Stop it," she said. "You have no right to fuck with me like this. I don't want your fake love or your little games. I control all of this, and I don't even know why. It's who I am, and it's what I do." She leaned forward, really pissed. "I hate my life. I just wanted to have a child and to be left alone. Why don't you hate me? You should hate me now."

"I don't hate anyone, Lexi. I never have. You know that. You knew that when I married you. Plus, you're the mother of my children. I can't hate you."

"Just Charlotte, you asshole. Shelby isn't even yours. You are meaningless and a red herring, all in one. God, why can't you understand your purpose? Grovel, grovel, grovel, gone. Why won't you leave!"

"What's wrong? What have I done?"

"I don't need anyone," Lexi said, standing up. "I can ruin you, and I don't need the girls anymore. All your reasons for existing are done. So if you want to fuck with me, I can end all this. You exist at my pleasure. This isn't stickball and hockey sticks. This is real life, you bastard. Garbage in, garbage out. Do you understand me?"

"No. I'm sorry, I don't. I have no idea what you're talking about, Lexi. I think you're drunk."

"Do you understand me now, Daddy!" Lexi yelled, grabbing his hair.

"I almost punched her. I wanted to badly. It hurts when someone pulls your hair. But nothing good would've come from it, so I composed myself."

"Sure, I understand you," Travis answered.

"I'll take the girls away if you make me, I don't care," she said, giving me a sarcastic air-kiss, then she let go of his hair and walked toward the door. "Pleasant dreams, unless I change my mind. Horror stories always end up in a house, and nobody cares. They just keep building them, bigger and bigger." She turned and glared at me again. "Death doesn't scare me, but you do. You better watch out. I'll fuck you up."

"She walked downstairs, got in her car and drove away. I have no idea where. That evening she came home like normal, acting like nothing happened.

"I never made her coffee again."

"What did it all mean that night, Travis? What was Lexi trying to say?"

"I have no idea," Travis said, taking a big swig from his drink. "But it definitely was the first time I noticed that Lexi was losing it."

Chapter 10

Tough Questions

"Were you scared of Lexi?" Ava asked.

"Scared? Oh, I don't know. I was scared that she would divorce me and I would lose my girls. I had no money to fight her with in court, all the divorce laws were against me because I was a man, and she was a lawyer. I'd be screwed in a court of law if she dumped me."

"No, I mean did you feel like you were in danger, physically?"

"I didn't lock my bedroom door at night, if that's what you mean."

"So Lexi never hit you or the girls?"

"Before her birthday party, not really. She slapped me if I screwed up or said the wrong thing, but not every night or anything. And she was never around the girls before that night. Hell, sometimes Lexi forgot her own daughters' names."

"How about after that night?" Ava asked.

"Lexi was more physical. The girls were afraid of her."

"Did she hit the girls?"

"Not a lot. It was more like disciplining them. If there were toys on the ground that were no longer being played with, she spanked them. If they didn't hear Lexi or did directions wrong, Lexi would pick them up, yell at them and shake them. If the girls laughed and Lexi didn't know why, or worse, if she thought they were laughing at her because she was drunk or something, Lexi would slap them."

"Why Travis? What was the change after that night?"

"Lexi was just pissed." Travis sat back, trying to arrange his thoughts. "I think Lexi thought things at home were going to be different. She wanted chaos and misery. She wanted me to be unhappy as a caregiver and utterly dependent on her in every way. But I didn't break, and worse, I wanted to be her friend instead of hating her.

"She wanted the girls to be a mess, but the girls were polite, well-kept, and smart for their ages. Both learned to read by age four. They were thoughtful, kind and good little Christian girls. So Lexi felt wronged, unneeded, and unappreciated."

"I don't understand," Ava said.

"Welcome to my world."

"Welcome to my world?" Ava asked, frustrated. "What does that even mean, Travis?"

"It means maybe I'm wrong. Maybe Lexi was mad at something else. Maybe she didn't care about the girls or me. I truly had no idea, Ava. I was living with madness. Her madness and I had no idea what was going on. Nothing made sense, and I'm trying to explain that to you. I didn't know how to make her happy or help her, and I had no power to do so. I couldn't commit her, I couldn't run away, and I couldn't kill her. I had to protect my girls and survive. That was all I could do in my situation, a situation that I had entered into willingly. I asked Lexi to marry me, and now I had to face the consequences that came with such a horrible mistake. And I didn't want to ruin my daughters' lives because of my big mistake."

"You thought about killing Lexi?"

"No, I was just explaining to you—," Travis said, a little embarrassed, realizing what he had said. "Look, I was trapped, and I was just saying that it was not an option. I didn't want to kill her, but it would've ended the madness. No, I never thought about killing her." He grabbed Ava's hand. "I never wanted to kill her. I just wanted it to end."

Chapter 11

————◆————

The Chance

"So then, out of nowhere, a week after Lexi's birthday, Kevin asked me to play golf."

"Play golf?" Ava asked. "Who's Kevin?"

"The father of Anna, Charlotte's best friend at school. On a Tuesday morning, as I was dropping the kids off at school, Kevin asked if I played golf and if I could play in a scramble with his team that morning. One of his partners had canceled the night before, and he needed a body. It was all paid for, and it was at Memorial Park."

"No way. Memorial Park. You played, right?"

"I said that I had to pick up the girls after school so I couldn't play, but he said his wife could pick up my girls and she would take care of them. Charlotte already had a play-date at Anna's home before and said it was a blast, so this was a legitimate answer. I was a little worried leaving Shelby there also, she being only four years old and not having a child her age at their house. But I decided to go for it and said yes, I'd play. I raced home, changed, and found my clubs in the attic. I got to the course and had only thirty minutes to warm-up. Gently swinging so I wouldn't get hurt after a six-year lay-off, I couldn't believe what was happening."

"What Travis?"

"My swing was perfect," he answered, staring right into her eyes, with a knowing smile that she had never seen before. "You see, my swing was pretty good when I stopped six years ago, but I had a fatal flaw, especially under pressure: I brought the club back too far on my backswing when I got excited or tried too hard, so I'd get stuck at the top and hit a weak fade. Under pressure, I had to intentionally stop my backswing short, which was tough to repeat. It was my biggest weakness, and I was always fighting it when a match got tense or close. It felt natural to swing hard when my adrenaline flowed, and sometimes I couldn't resist going too far back. It kept me from being a consistent high-level golfer.

"But now, after the layoff, I was less limber on my takeaway. I think holding an infant on my right shoulder all those years lessened my range of motion, making me take the club back to my perfect swing position instead of too far, so my swing was, well, it was perfect. After twenty minutes, I was swinging a golf club better than I ever had in my life. I ran off the range, hit a few putts and couldn't wait to hit the course.

"So you're a 25 handicap now, huh?" a voice said out of nowhere.

"I turned, and it was my old buddy Glenn, the head pro at Memorial Park. We hugged and caught up real quick. I explained that Kevin had never played golf with me before, that I was a late addition this morning, and I had no idea that he had written me down as a 25 handicap. We both laughed, he wrote me down as a scratch, and we promised to catch up after the round.

"I played lights out that day. I can't tell you how much fun it was: relaxing on a weekday, the smell of the grass, the feeling of hitting a golf ball, and the enjoyment of adult male company. Kevin spent the whole day getting drunk and bragging to his buddies about how he had brought me and what a genius he was. By the end of the round, everyone was playing well. We shot 17 under, and with their handicaps, we won the tournament easily. I fell in love with golf all over again. This time harder."

"You really hadn't hit a golf ball for six years?" Ava asked.

"Physically, no," Travis answered, obviously proud. "But mentally, I had played thousands of rounds in my mind. Hell, I practiced every night in my dreams. You'd think that wouldn't matter, but it helped immensely. Maybe it was just getting older and the natural maturity as you age, but I can't tell you how relaxed I was on a golf course now. I hadn't hit a golf ball in six years, but I felt like a seasoned veteran who hadn't missed a day.

"It's funny. I read a story a few years ago about an American POW who played golf in his mind while he was imprisoned. As a kid, he belonged to a country club and loved playing golf, so to escape his misery in captivity, he played his home course every day in his mind for hours. He literally would play different shots on different days, and hit from different tees, experimenting and working on his game in his mind to stay sane. After they rescued him and he came home safely, he played his home course and shot even par for the first time. Maybe that was like what happened to me in some way, I don't know, but I did come back mentally stronger."

"So we got our trophies at the awards dinner, and after, I continued to catch up with Glenn. I explained to him that it was my first round in six years, that I had a blast, but I was trapped right now with my daughters."

"Can you escape for the Houston City Amateur in late September?" Glenn asked. "It's almost two months away. You can train here for free. The guys really miss you, we all do, and we'd love to see you playing again. What can I do to help?"

"You're great, Glenn. But I don't have time for the qualifier, and it would be almost impossible to escape for a long weekend to play the Houston Amateur."

"Don't worry about the qualifier, I'll take care of that," Glenn said. "You're in right now. And one of the boys will pay your entry fee. You just figure out a way to get off that Friday through Sunday for the tournament."

"So I start sneaking out to practice during the week. I woke up early and did my house chores, getting as much done as I could, then I would head out to Memorial Park and practice golf for about four hours, sometimes a little longer. It took a month for my short game to come back. Slowly, the touch did return, and my contact was cleaner than before I had stopped playing. Even my putting improved. I think my tighter swing took pressure off my putting, making me feel like I didn't have to sink everything, so I was releasing the putter head with ease and hitting my lines, therefore draining more putts. By the first week in September, I was ready for the Houston City Amateur, but I still had to figure out how to get away for that tournament weekend.

"That was when I decided to go for it. I called Lexi's favorite resort in Galveston and asked for a deal on the weekend of the tournament. Because they were loyal customers, the resort said that Lexi and the girls could get a penthouse suite for a regular rate, especially since they were ordering a nanny. I said it sounded great, and I booked it. That night, when Lexi came home, I ambushed her.

"Hey, Lexi. I did something today. I hope it was all right."

"What the fuck did you do?" Lexi asked, tired and obviously loaded.

"The Ambassador Resort and Spa in Galveston called and said they had a special rate for you and the girls. You could get a penthouse suite at a regular rate, and your favorite nanny can take the girls all weekend. It's for late September, the 27th through the 30th."

"The Ambassador called you?" Lexi asked. "Why didn't they call me?"

"Good question," I said, cornered. "I have no idea. Maybe the Ambassador couldn't reach you on your phone this morning. Or—. Or, maybe you told them my phone number. Am I your emergency phone number in their registry? Maybe they called the emergency number by accident. Anyway, it was a one day offer, so I said yes."

"You accepted! Why didn't you call me first?"

"You were at work. I didn't want to bother you. Plus, it was too good a deal."

"Fuck me," Lexi scoffed. "When is this? The end of September?"

"27th through the 30th."

"I guess it's ok," Lexi said, heading upstairs. "Call me next time. Don't be such a child."

"I said I was sorry again, then silently cheered as she disappeared on the staircase."

"Travis," Ava asked, "what if you had gotten caught? What if Lexi found out that you made the reservation yourself? What would she have done?"

"I didn't get caught. And I know, looking back, I can't believe I made the reservation. I put my life and my children's lives at risk of being broken apart. I know. But I needed to play in that golf tournament. I can't explain it. The past month had been the greatest escape of my life, and I just wanted to keep it going. It was irrational and juvenile, thinking that I could get away with this and nothing would happen. But I had to try, and for some reason, I thought that I could pull it off. I convinced myself that Lexi would never know."

"It just seems so risky, Travis, especially knowing the girls would be left with Lexi if you got caught. You even said the girls were scared of her and she had abused them in the past."

"I know, I know," Travis said, motioning Mac for another round. "It was selfish and stupid. But I just had to try and play. I can't even tell you why. Just something inside. I had to play."

Chapter 12

The City Amateur

"So a couple of weeks later, Lexi and the girls left for Galveston on that Thursday afternoon. The next morning, I drove to Memorial Park for the Houston City Amateur, prepared and ready to show it. I had a great warm-up and couldn't wait to start.

"The first round was pretty standard. I played with a guy who was woefully nervous and hitting it all over the place on the first few holes, and his score showed it, but I got him to calm down, and he ended up shooting 83. I shot even par on the front, then snuck three birdies on the back. I drove it well, but my irons could've been sharper. My mind kinda' wandered during the round, not used to the grind. Some guy named Raleigh Durham shot six under and had a three-stroke lead over me.

"The next day, the second round, it was wet and windy. A big test. I had to get up and down from off the green seven times during the round, made bogey twice and birdied twice, all pars on the rest. I shot a respectable even par on that miserable day. I couldn't help my partner in this weather. He completely lost it mentally and shot 92. It was that tough a day for almost everybody.

"But that Raleigh guy, the leader, shot two under. He had a five-stroke lead over me. The guy in third was seven strokes behind me, so it was a two-man tournament now.

"Sunday was the last day, thirty-six holes, two rounds in one day, five strokes back. I don't know why, but they always play thirty-six holes on that last day. The good news was that gave me a lot of time to make up five strokes.

"That night, while I was eating at home alone, a feeling came over me. It was like an adrenaline-laced calm or something, like my senses were heightened for no reason. I was so ready to play all night. I kept thinking about that first tee shot. I knew I was going to win."

"You knew?" Ava asked.

"Cocky-bastard," Mac interrupted, dropping off some fresh drinks. Instead of leaving, he pulled up a chair to listen in.

"Yeah, I knew," Travis said, loving his fresh Jack and Sprite Zero. "The next morning, the rain had stopped, the temperature was warm, and the course had dried out, so the conditions were perfect. I finally got to meet Raleigh because we were playing partners now. Nice guy, tall, with a long fluid swing. Raleigh was pretty cool at first.

"We both started out hot. I shot four-under on the front nine, and Raleigh shot three-under. We were having a good time, talking and joking with each other. But on the back nine, Raleigh's putter went a little cold and mine stayed hot. I had four more birds on the back, and he shot two over."

"You shot a 64," Ava laughed, "and Raleigh shot 71. You had a two-stroke lead now with 18 holes to go. Was Raleigh surprised?"

"Raleigh was pissed. All of a sudden, he didn't want to talk any-more, which was fine with me.

"So we take a thirty-minute break before the last round, then we head to the first tee, and I get a great surprise. About fifty of my old buddies showed up to watch my final eighteen holes. Glenn probably called them. They gave me this great ovation as I walked to the first tee. I looked over at Raleigh, and he was shaken up by it all, com-pletely out of it mentally. The tournament was over, and we hadn't even teed off on the first hole yet.

"I had a great front nine, showing off for all my buddies and laughing with them, but Raleigh couldn't hold it together. The poor guy tried to dig deep, but nothing was there. I basically played the same front as the morning round. Raleigh shot a 41, and I shot a 32 again.

"You had an eleven stroke lead at the turn," Ava said, shaking her head.

"On the back nine, Raleigh and I became friends again. He real-ized that I was a good guy, and I was very respectful to him, clapping for almost every one of his shots. Even my buddies started cheering for him a little. He shot two under on the back, finishing strong. I can't tell you how cool he was when he shook my hand after the round. Raleigh ended up being a great guy."

"What did you shoot on the back nine?" Ava asked.

"I get up on the tenth tee," Travis said, "and guess who I see. Mac."

"That's right," Mac said, grinning. "On Saturday, a guy at work told me that Travis was in the paper, that he was playing in the Houston City Amateur. Sunday morning, I read on the sports page that Travis was in second place, so for the first time ever, I called in sick, skipped work and went to watch my old buddy play golf. I tried to hide in the background, but Travis finally caught sight of me on the tenth tee. Travis ran over, gave me this big hug, and we started catching up for a few minutes, but he had to go finish the round. So I asked him to show me what he's got on the back nine. That son-of-a-bitch shot six-under!"

"You shot a 62 in the final round of the Houston City Amateur?" Ava asked. "You never told me about shooting 62 in the final round. You went 64-62 on Sunday. You won by—. So you won by 15 strokes."

"I played well," Travis said, with a wry smile. "So I got the trophy and raced home. My girls arrived a couple of hours before me, and Lexi was pissed that I wasn't home. But I had planned it out already. I told her that I tried to buy some azalea bushes, to fix some of the front beds, but couldn't find them. Being devious, I had some azalea bushes already in the garage, pre-bought for her to see. I told her that I suddenly realized that I didn't have enough azaleas, so I went to some other nurseries that evening, to find a few more, but none of the nurseries had the white azalea bushes that she liked."

"Whatever," Lexi responded, already drunk and headed upstairs. "Our bags are in the car. And take a shower. You smell awful. Worse than normal."

Chapter 13

The Newspaper

"The next morning, everything blew up. I was planting the azalea bushes in the front beds, when, out of nowhere, Lexi raced down the driveway in her Mercedes toward the garage. She never came home early on a weekday. I went to see what was up and there she was, opening my car trunk and throwing my golf clubs on the ground.

"You stupid bastard!" Lexi yelled, walking toward me now. "You have no idea what you've done."

"Lexi, all I did was play in a little golf tournament while y'all were gone. It was nothing."

"You lied to me!" Lexi screamed, then slapped my face. Hard. "You made me look like a fool. You made the reservations for Galveston, didn't you? You've been playing golf all along. I trusted you. But all you've done is ruin your own life, not mine."

"Then Lexi stormed toward her Mercedes, reached in the car and grabbed a newspaper, throwing it at my feet.

"You are finished," she said, walking in the back door.

"I picked up the paper and on the front of the sports section was a big picture of me, under the headline, '*The Best That Never Was*.'"

"It was my fault," Mac interrupted. "Well, me and some other guys. After Travis left with his trophy, a reporter followed me to my car. He saw Travis talking to me and guessed we were friends. I started telling the reporter all about Travis, how he was this great prodigy who gave it all up for his wife and kids. I guess it made me feel like a big shot or something, talking to some reporter, so I went on forever. I knew better. But I wanted to brag about my buddy. The reporter also interviewed the pro at Memorial Park. What's his name?"

"Glenn," Ava and Travis said at the same time.

"Right," Mac said. "Glenn bragged about Travis, too. The reporter interviewed like twenty other muni-guys, and they all had great stories about Travis's exploits. The article made Travis sound like a golf hero, the guy who gave up his golf future for his wife and kids, to make sure his family was happy and all their dreams came true. It was a great article."

"But Lexi didn't like it," Travis said. "She had portrayed herself as the woman who didn't need a man or any help in her life. Or, to some, she portrayed herself as a single woman who was not married. So an article calling her married with kids, or needing help from a man, was a complete insult to her stated reality to others. In other words, she felt the article was calling her a liar. And it was."

"I've got people at work running up to me all morning," Lexi said, as she paced around the living room, drinking scotch, "asking if you were my husband and telling me how lucky I was, how they had no idea that I had such a devoted husband. Telling me, me, how lucky I was! One little bastard asked if I could get you to sign his newspaper. And I hadn't even read the article yet and had no fucking idea what the hell was going on because you fucking lied to me. I had to leave my office, on a Monday at 10:00 am, because of you and your lies, you fucking bastard!"

"Lexi reached up to slap my face, but I caught her wrist before her hand hit me. I wouldn't let her slap again."

"Oh, that's assault, you bastard," Lexi said, grinning. "You can never lay a hand on a woman. Now you've done it. I want you out of here. Do you understand me? You're finished. I want you to go upstairs, pack up your shit and get the hell out of here. I want a divorce, and I'm getting the girls. If you fight me in any way, I will file for a restraining order against you, and your abuse, and you will never see the girls again. And don't you think that I won't do it! I've done it before, and I will do it again. I am leaving for one hour, and you better be gone by the time I get back. If you are still here, I will call the police, and I will make sure that you spend at least one night in jail, you lying bastard. You did it this time. We are over!"

"Lexi left, so I grabbed a bunch of garbage bags, packed up my clothes and left. I parked at the end of the street, to see if she came home in an hour, and she did, followed by a locksmith. Lexi had all the locks changed instantly.

"I know I should've been scared or whatever, about my situation, but all I could think about was Charlotte and Shelby, and how I wouldn't be there to pick them up from school. Maybe ever again."

Chapter 14

Helpless

"I drove around for a couple of hours, trying to figure out what was the best thing for me to do now, but I came up with nothing. Finally, I drove over to Marcos, the restaurant I used to work at, and waited for Mac to show up for the night shift. Mac parked, saw me walking toward him, looking like a lost dog, and he knew what had happened immediately."

"I had read the paper that morning," Mac interjected, "and couldn't believe how big an article it was. I thought it was going to be a little blurb on the back page or something. When I saw Travis walking up, head down and shattered, I knew that he hadn't told Lexi about playing in the tournament and we had ruined everything for him."

"It was all me, Mac, I screwed up," Travis said, sternly, as Mac left to go back to work on the bar area. "Mac gave me the keys to his apartment, and I started living there with him."

"What about the girls?" Ava asked. "What did Lexi do with them?"

"Lexi was a smart woman. She called the nanny from Galveston, paid her to come to Houston and be a live-in nanny. Her name was Jenny, and she left Galveston that night. Lexi had her move into my room, like I was just a memory. $1,500 a week, plus room and board. Not a bad gig. Lexi's world barely changed, so she was happy.

"Mac got home after his shift, and we brainstormed. Having saved a little over the years, Mac gave me five-grand, all the money that he had in the world, for a lawyer. Knowing a lawyer friend from golf, I called him, and he referred me to some high-powered guy who met with me the next day. It cost three-grand for the initial visit. The lawyer said he'd do a background check on Lexi and her finances, to see what position I was in for a divorce settlement, and more importantly, how I could get custody of my girls.

"About three days later, the lawyer called back to explain that I was screwed. His private investigator discovered that Lexi had been married twice before and claimed spousal abuse in both cases. She was an expert at it. They talked to one of her ex-husbands, and he said just run away, as far as possible."

"Why?" Ava asked.

"The ex-husband claimed that he tried to limit her half of the divorce settlement, because of her mental abuse, and because she had her successful job, making almost as much as him. Out of the blue, Lexi invited him over to the house, just to talk. He drove over, knocked on her door, and she ran out, screaming, her face all bloody and her nightgown torn apart. Lexi flagged down a car in the middle of the road and told the driver that her ex-husband had beaten her up and tried to rape her. The guy went to jail for six months."

"Oh, my God."

"Yeah. So the lawyer said because of the type of woman that I married, and my limited finances to fight her in court, it was best if I just settled with her and didn't fight for custody. So there I was, three-grand poorer and knowing what I already had known. I was screwed.

"Then, a week later, out of nowhere, Mac came home from work and said Glenn needed to talk to me, that he had stopped by Marcos and said it was important. So I head over to Memorial Park the next day."

"I got you into the Houston Open!" Glenn said, so excited. "You are going to play in a PGA tournament. I talked to the Houston Golf Association, and they all agreed. They knew your story from the paper and thought it would be great publicity. You're getting a special exemption."

"Are you serious?"

"Yes! The Houston Open is moving to a new course this year, Deer Run Golf Club, so they're looking for cool stories for advertising. What could be better than a gifted local muni-guy living out his dream? '*Come out and watch, Houston. Local Boy does good. Bring the whole family.*'"

"What do I have to do?"

"Practice. You got six months to prepare. I got you free privileges at Deer Run, on the range and the course. I can get you a sponsor. Me! No money, but I'll get you free clothes, balls, and gloves. It'll all have the Memorial Park Golf Course logo on them. You'll be a muni-golfing god! But there is one catch. Just one. To get the free stuff, you have to turn pro."

"No problem, I don't care. Glenn, is this for real?"

"Travis, this is a new course. No one on tour has ever seen it. You get to practice on it for six months. Travis, you can win this."

Chapter 15

Fear

"I tried to care about the Houston Open, but all I could think about was my girls."

"Did you have any contact with them at all?" Ava asked.

"None. The Pastor at their school watched them for me. I told him my situation and asked him to look after them while they were there. He would give me weekly updates, but I explained that he could not mention me at all to Charlotte or Shelby, no matter what the girls asked or said."

"Why?"

"Because the girls could not say anything new about me to Lexi or she might go nuts. I was not allowed to have any contact with them, in any form or way. Ever. Her rules."

"What would Lexi do if they said they saw you?"

"I didn't know, and I didn't want to find out."

Chapter 16

Survival

"So what did you do, Travis?" Ava asked.

"The only thing I could. I became a full-time golfer. I'd drive out to Deer Run Golf Club every morning, worked on my game all day, then I'd drive to Marco's for dinner. I ate for free thanks to Mac. The consistent routine helped my training.

"Deer Run was difficult, a mixture of old and new designs, with a staggering length, 7,600 yards. But the length was deceiving because if you could drive the ball long and high, you could bite off a lot of the distance on a few holes, especially the par fives by carrying the trees. The greens were slick, and the rough was light, just like the Masters, because The Houston Open was always the lead-up tournament to The Masters. Players liked how Houston made the conditions similar to the major, so it was for a great warm-up week for The Masters, therefore always attracting a strong field of players. Prior knowledge helped on a course like Deer Run, and I got to know it like the back of my hand.

"But I missed my girls. I couldn't take it anymore, so I called Lexi at work."

"Hello, Travis," Lexi said, matter-of-factly. "I suppose you're looking for money."

"No, not at all. I just wanted to check in with you. I assume you and the girls are ok?"

"Never better."

"Lexi, I've done everything you wanted for the past three months. I've stayed away from you and the girls and caused no trouble. I just wanted to know if I could have the girls for a day since I am their father. It doesn't have to be a holiday or anything, and I don't want the visit to bother you at all. How about I take the girls to the zoo one Saturday so you can relax?"

"Obviously you could give a shit about seeing me," Lexi said. "You just want to see the girls, huh?"

"No. If you would like to come, that would be great. Of course, I miss you also."

"Oh, shut your face. First of all, only one of the girls is your biological daughter. And I don't know if I can trust you because you are a convicted liar."

"A reformed and regretful liar," Travis said, graciously, "who wants to prove himself to you again."

"Fine. I will bring Charlotte, your only daughter, to the park at noon on Saturday. You can talk to her for ten minutes, under my supervision. That is if she wants to talk to you. If she doesn't then you'll know why we never showed."

"Lexi hung up the phone," Travis said, motioning Mac for another round.

"Charlotte would want to talk to you, right?" Ava asked.

"Yeah, of course. That was just Lexi being Lexi."

Chapter 17

The Reunion

"Daddy!" Charlotte said, running toward Travis.

"Hey, little girl," Travis said, bending down to hug her. "You grew again."

"She's done a lot of things since you abandoned us," Lexi said. "You look tan. Still playing golf like a bum, I see. God knows you don't have a real job."

"Hey, Lexi. Good to see you. You look great."

"Oh, shut your face. I'm going to sit in the car. You got only five minutes because I need to leave pronto after your prison yard visit for an important meeting. Adult stuff that you wouldn't understand. You try anything, and you'll be in jail by midnight."

"She misses you," Charlotte said, as they watched Lexi walk away. "She talks about you when she's drinks a lot. Almost every night."

"Well, I miss you guys. How is Shelby?"

"Shelby's ok. I protect her. She doesn't know how to stay out of trouble cuz she's a little girl. But I keep her good."

"Good girl. What should you do if Mommy starts acting mean?"

"Cough and pretend to be sick, and she'll stay away," Charlotte answered, smiling. "When are you coming home?"

"I don't know, little girl. I may not be allowed to come home. But I'm going to try and win some money so you can live with me. I need money to get us away from Mommy."

"How can you win money?" Charlotte asked.

"I got invited to play in a golf tournament. If I play well, I can win some money."

"I don't know, Daddy," Charlotte said, starting to cry. "That sounds hard. Why don't you say you're sorry so you can come home again? It's not fun when you're gone."

"Mommy doesn't want me home, Charlotte. If she did, I'd be there right now."

"I hate Mommy. I know I shouldn't, but God's wrong. I love my Daddy, and I hate my Mommy."

"Charlotte, keep protecting Shelby. She needs you. Just stay out of trouble. I will do everything that I can to be with y'all again. I promise. I'm trying to figure a way out of this, but it's tough to fix."

"I miss you, Daddy."

"I miss you, little girl. So much it hurts."

"Shelby wanted to see you. She cried when she had to stay home." Charlotte wiped her nose and tried to smile. "I lost another tooth."

"Wow! Another one. Top or bottom?"

"Bottom."

"Open up and show me."

"Time's up," Lexi said, sneaking up on them and grabbing Charlotte's hand. "Bye."

"Wait. I need to show Daddy how I lost a tooth."

"Nobody cares," Lexi said, yanking her arm and walking away. "Especially him."

"They walked to Lexi's car, then drove away," Travis said, a little teary-eyed. "That was the toughest five minutes of my life."

Chapter 18

————◆————

The Plan

"I tried to practice, but it was tough after seeing Charlotte. The next few months were a blur. It rained a lot, so it was hard to make a consistent practice routine. I did what I could, but it was lonely, and everything in my life seemed pointless. I kept kicking myself for playing in that stupid city amateur, and I couldn't figure out how playing in the Houston Open would fix anything. I should've been home with my girls. I let them down. But the Houston Open was the only thing in my life at that time, so I kept training.

"All of a sudden, it was here. The week of the tournament. Out of nowhere, Deer Run stopped being a golf club and turned into a sports complex. Sponsor tents and scaffolding were everywhere. Giant television cranes were scattered all over the course now. Crowds of people walking aimlessly, beer and restaurant stands dispersed on every hole, and all the guys that I'd seen on television were playing on my course now. There was always a strong field of players at the Houston Open; eight out of the top ten were there that year. To say that I was intimidated would be an understatement.

"On Monday, players could play a practice round. Glenn drove with me to the course, wanting to see it all himself. He gave me my player's packet, with my player's badge, rules, and itinerary. We figured out how to check in, found out all the places that I could go, then headed out to the course to play the front nine. It was fun, just playing and walking with Glenn, talking about all the memories through the years, and trying to accept that I was now playing in the Houston Open. Glenn had a blast, but I was happy when we left. The next day, Tuesday, I practiced a little at Deer Run, then played a practice round on the back nine by myself. Crowds were getting bigger, so I left a little early. Wednesday, I just stayed home and rested. It was a little too much, you know what I mean?"

"I'll bet you were nervous," Ava said.

"More intimidated than nervous. I felt very out of place and not worthy of my position. I felt undeserving and overwhelmed. I had not paid my dues, and yet here I was. I started to realize that I was a prop, a marketing ploy, and others were more deserving than me, that I had taken someone's spot who truly deserved to be there. Does that make sense?"

"Yes. How did you deal with it?"

"I called my lawyer, asked him how much I needed to go to court with Lexi and have a chance at custody of the girls. He said $200k. I looked up the payouts for the Houston Open and figured out that fourth place paid $336k. After taxes, I needed to get at least fourth place to have a chance for my kids.

"So I set my goal on fourth place. It became my world and my only thought. I needed fourth to get my kids back."

"That's not what you taught me," Ava said. "You taught me to let the game come to you. You said let go, and you'll play your best golf."

"Right," Travis said, downing his Jack and Sprite Zero. "I learned that lesson on Thursday."

Chapter 19

────◆────

The First Round

"The first round. I teed off at 11:30 am. I tried to get there early, but I forgot about the traffic. Cars were everywhere. I had never been to a PGA event and didn't realize how many people came out to watch. Plus, when I tried to park at the club, the guy didn't believe that I was a player. He called his supervisor to make sure I was legit. It was a nightmare. So instead of having two hours to prepare, I had less than an hour.

"I went to check in, and they asked for my caddy's name."

"I don't have a caddy. I'm carrying my bag."

"Sorry, sir," the official said. "Every player has to have a caddy. It's the rules."

"I couldn't believe it. So I ask the guy if he knew anyone. He made a call and said a player had withdrawn with a rib injury and his caddy said he'd loop for me, that he would meet me on the range.

"So I ran out to the range, tried to warm up a little, then this guy walked up and stared at me hitting balls."

"Are you Travis Hatfield?" he asked

"Yes, sir."

"I'm Randy. They asked me to caddy for you. Do you think you'll make the cut?"

"Uh, yeah, I think so."

"Well, I could go to Acapulco with some old buddies this week-end. I'm already packed. Just tell me. Are you for real or what? I don't want to waste a couple days when I could party with friends. You know?"

"I'll do my best," Travis said, "but I really do need a caddy. If you can't, I'll find somebody else."

"You won't punk out on me?" Randy asked, a little wishy-washy.

"I'll do my best."

"Ok, I'll do it. I get 10%. Just make sure the bag is light."

"So we head to the first tee, and I was super tight. I hadn't done my normal warm-up, and I hated my caddy. They announced my name to tee off, and Randy was MIA. I look behind me, and he was sitting on a bench with my clubs, thirty feet away, eating a sandwich. I had to jog over to him and grab my driver. He said sorry and laughed. I drove it down the middle, but fatted a wedge on my approach, barely hit the green, and left myself a forty-footer for birdie. Then I choked the putt, leaving it six feet short. I started lining up the par putt, when, out of nowhere, Randy stuck his head in and said it broke right."

"It's straight," I said.

"That breaks right," Randy said, knowingly. "You're wrong."

"I look again, see nothing, but I play it outside left. It rolled straight and lipped out."

"You pulled it," Randy said, disgusted.

"The next hole, I had another six-footer for par. I read it alone and lipped it out again."

"You pulled that one, too," Randy said, shaking his head.

"We barely talked the rest of the round. Every once in a while, Randy would say something like '*I could be in Acapulco*' or '*At least it's not raining.*' I made two more bogeys, but I also had an eagle on the eleventh hole. I shot +2, and the leader was at −7. Randy left my bag on the ground, without even saying bye.

"I played pretty well, but mentally, I took myself completely out of that round. I put too much pressure on each shot, playing for fourth place, and didn't play my game. I didn't trust myself and let Randy get to me. It was, by far, the most miserable round of my life."

"Did you think the tournament was over?" Ava asked.

"I knew it was over," Travis said. "I didn't want to come back on Friday. I had let everyone down and felt completely out of place. That night, I knew the tournament and my life was over."

"There was nothing positive about the whole day?"

"Not really. No, there was one great thing about that day. Greg Mathers, the pro who I played with for the first two rounds. He was an older journeyman golfer, and a great guy to be paired with anytime. He was amazing the whole first round, keeping me positive and not letting me give up. Greg shot −4 and was a pleasure to watch. I probably would've shot +10 if he hadn't been there."

"I remember him," Ava said, smiling.

"After the round, when we shook hands, I told him how much I appreciated his encouragement and how much I enjoyed watching him play, that I had learned a lot from him that day."

"No problem," Greg said. "You have a great swing. Tomorrow will be your day."

"I felt lucky to have played with Greg that day and Friday, and I knew he was the reason that I was able to hold it together that first round. I wanted to pay him back on Friday, by making sure Greg had a great round, no matter what happened to me."

"So you were no longer playing for that fourth place nonsense?" Ava asked, poking him a little.

"Right," Travis said, laughing. "I'd learned my lesson. I was going to forget all that fourth place nonsense, try to play golf my way and maybe even have some fun."

Chapter 20

----◆----

The Second Round

"Well, you know all about the second round, so we can skip that," Travis said.

"Are you crazy?" Ava asked, astonished. "I was only six years old. I remember bits and pieces, but certainly not everything. Plus, I want to hear it from your perspective."

"She's right, Ke-mo sah-bee," Mac said, reloading drinks and sitting down again. "I've never heard you talk about it either. Hell, nobody has. Ever. I've been waiting all afternoon for this."

"Just watch it on YouTube," Travis said, grabbing his fresh libation.

"We can't see the front nine, Travis," Ava said, making sure the microphone was in perfect position. "Television coverage hadn't come on yet. You have to tell us about the front nine, and everything."

"Fine. But what are we doing for dinner?"

"I can't believe you're still hungry," Ava said. "You ate a whole pizza."

"I'll cook something later," Mac said, settling in. "Stop stalling and start talking."

Travis sighed, took a big swig, then organized his thoughts.

"I got to the course early on Friday for my 12:20 pm tee time. Taking my time, I had a great warm-up. My irons were sharp, and I knew it could be a special day. For some reason, I had almost forgotten about the first round. It was amazing. But my caddy, Randy, hadn't changed. He showed up ten minutes before my tee time, I swear a little loaded. I couldn't believe it."

"So maybe we can make the cut," Randy said, grabbing my bag and heading to the first tee.

"I got on the first tee, and I shook hands with good-old Greg Mathers. I told him to play well."

"Let's make it a special day," Greg said, patting me on the back.

"I drilled a drive right down the middle, pulled out my sand wedge and pure'd it, right at the pin, but the son of a gun hit the pin, bounced hard and rolled twenty-five feet right. If it had missed that pin, I would've had a five-footer for birdie, at most. Really sucked, but I tried to regroup. I lined-up the twenty-five-footer, stroked it, and it caught a lot of cup, but the ball just didn't drop. Might've been the best putt I hit all week, but it just didn't fall."

"Man, you are snake-bit," Randy said, putting the pin back in. "Lucky me."

"So we head to the second hole, and there was a bit of a wait to tee off. The fairway finally cleared and I was lining up my drive, when I saw this shadow bobbing back and forth near my ball. Some guy in the crowd wouldn't stand still, and his shadow was everywhere. I was about to say something, when the guy groaned, crashed through the ropes and fell face-first on the tee box. He was having a heart attack. Greg rolled him over and tried to help him. I yelled for a doctor and tried to help Greg. I've never felt so useless. Some guy in the crowd, I'm not sure if he was a doctor or what, started pumping his hands on the guy's chest, then giving him mouth to mouth. He said that he felt a pulse and everyone cheered. I looked up and saw a woman and a little girl crying. They obviously belonged to the dying man.

"An ambulance arrived a few minutes later, and the paramedics worked on the man for almost twenty minutes. The guy even started talking a little. It was great. They got him on a gurney and into the ambulance, then the wife and the child started to board the ambulance, but the paramedics said no."

"I'm sorry ma'am. We can only take one rider."

"But I have to go with him, and I can't leave my daughter here."

"All of a sudden, the dying man yelled for his wife, then went into cardiac arrest again. A paramedic said she had to make a decision now. I don't know why, but I ran toward the woman."

"I can take your daughter."

"What?" the woman asked, stunned.

"I can take your daughter. You take care of your husband. I'm a stay-at-home dad with two young daughters. I promise she'll be fine. You just take care of him. You've got to go. Don't worry, she's fine."

"She stared at me for a second, then jumped in the ambulance, and they were gone.

"I turned to look at the little girl, and she was in tears, scared out of her mind. It hit me right then that her mother never even told her goodbye. I slowly walked up to her and bent down.

"Hi. My name is Mr. Hatfield. I'm so sorry about your father, and I'm sorry your mom had to leave, but I'm here for you. We are going to get through this together. Again, I'm Mr. Hatfield. What is your name?"

"Ava," the little girl said, in between tears. "You're a golfer. My dad likes you."

"That's right. I'm a golfer. Do I know your dad?"

"No," Ava said, then started to cry again.

"What the hell is going on?" Randy asked. "We can't take care of a kid. We're playing in a PGA tournament, for Christ-sakes."

"I realized that he had a point, and I may have crossed a huge line. I asked Greg if he minded having a little girl join our group."

"I'd be honored to have to her, and I'm even more honored to be playing with you," Greg answered instantly.

"Well, this is bullshit. I'm not caddying for a joke, and Travis, you're turning into a complete joke. Do you even want to make the cut?"

"You know what, Randy, you're right," I said. "You shouldn't caddy for me. Randy, you're fired. I just got a new caddy. Ava."

"You fucking asshole. You can't fire me."

"Then the coolest thing happened. Greg stepped up and cold-cocked Randy, a right to the jaw. The guy dropped like a stone."

"He said you're fired!" Gregg yelled, rubbing his now sore hand, then he composed himself. "Get off our tee box."

"Picking himself up, Randy spit on the ground, then walked off, never to be seen again."

"You ok?" Travis asked the little girl, wiping away a few of her tears.

"She shook her head yes. An official said it was time to play again. I told Ava to hold on for a second. I pulled my driver out of the bag, quickly lined it up, then swung.

"There was this tremendous roar from the crowd as my drive flew deep down the middle. It scared me when everyone erupted. Without noticing it, thousands of people surrounded us now. I mean thousands. The crowd had been so quiet as it grew, with everyone captivated by the heart attack, the little girl, and the punch. Plus, I was just focused on Ava and had forgotten about everything else.

"The whole gallery was emotionally attached to us now. Ava was like their child, and they all wanted to see was how I'd take care of her. They couldn't believe that I drove one straight, after a forty-five minute wait, and without even stretching or taking a practice swing. Greg clapped a little himself, laughing incredulously at the scene."

"This is really cool," he said, then he hit a nice drive himself that brought another tremendous roar.

"Ava, you're my caddy now," I said, placing my carry bag over my shoulders.

"Yes, sir. What does that mean?"

"First, it means you hold my hand as I walk," he said, reaching down, gently grabbing her little paw and starting to walk. "Then, I'm not sure. We will figure it all out as we go. Wait, I know. Second, you have to eat some ice cream."

"I saw this ice cream stand, Dipping Dots, on the other side of the ropes and we headed for it. She wanted cookies n' cream, I'll never forget. I tried to pull my wallet out to pay, but a gallery member beat me to it, so some random woman bought Ava the Dipping Dots. We headed back through the crowd, all of them clapping and giving us high-fives, and onto the course again. Greg had already hit, so I got to my ball, quickly lined it up and smoothed a nine iron, the ball softly landing eight feet from the cup. Do you remember that roar after that shot, Ava? It was amazing, just so loud. Greg applauded. What a great guy!

"So we got to the green. Greg two-putted for par. I started lining up my eight-footer, when Ava wandered onto the green with her ice cream, asking me what was going on. I told her that I was putting and I needed to hit the ball in that hole over there."

"Any advice?" Travis asked.

"Dad says don't leave a putt short, but I don't know what that means."

"It means your dad is a genius. That is great advice, little girl."

"So I lined it up, tapped it, and it gently rolled in for birdie. The crowd went wild. Even Ava went wild. She ran up and hugged me, carefully, not wanting to drop her Dipping Dots.

"Do that again," Ava said, smiling, with an ice cream mustache.

"Incredibly, I did birdie the next hole, but I got a par on the fourth hole. Ava got mad at the par and told me to try harder. On the fifth hole, the par five, both Greg and I hit the green in two. I had a twenty-footer for eagle and drained the sucker. The crowd went crazy, and Ava jumped into my arms. Then, from about fourteen feet, Greg nailed his eagle putt also. People went nuts again, and Ava jumped into Greg's arms! Greg literally started shedding a few tears. It was intense, just impossible to explain all the emotions that Greg and I had been through over the past two hours. And we still had thirteen holes to go.

"So we kept moving on. Greg made a few bogeys, but it was understandable. The noise and the people moving when he hit was terrible. They'd stay still and quiet for me, but as soon as I hit, they started running to see my next shot, not caring about Greg. But he was such a man and handled it with total class. You know, he never complained once. I swear, he enjoyed it. He was such a man. I par six, seven and eight, and I have no idea how I held it together. I think Ava grounded me and forced me to remain composed.

"Then the most amazing thing happened. Television coverage started at 3:00 pm and we became the main story on the course and in the world. The coverage began with Ava on my shoulders while I walked with my bag down the fairway, with the crowd singing '*John Jacob Jingleheimer Schmidt*.' See, there was a wait on the ninth hole tee box, and Ava got bored. So I asked her what her favorite song was, and she said that she and her father always sang '*John Jacob Jingleheimer Schmidt.*' Well, I had never heard the song before, so I asked her to sing it for me. She started singing this silly song in a little girl's voice. It was so precious. Then the crowd near the tee box started singing with her, cuz they all knew it. Evidently, everybody knew the song but me. After we tee off, everyone began serenading us as we walked off the box. Greg and his caddy were even singing. Ava got up on my shoulders and was leading the crowd like a conductor, thousands of people on both sides of the fairway, singing their hearts out. It was so cool. And that was when TV coverage started, right during that first serenade. A few holes later, when the TV audience learned that everyone was singing to make Ava feel better because her father had a heart attack on the second hole, all their hearts melted and the ratings went through the roof. It is still most watched round of golf during the week in the history of the PGA Tour. The rest of the day, every hole we went to, people sang that silly song, and it was amazing. Ava loved it. I birdied that ninth hole to shoot 31 on the front.

"So I made another eagle on eleven and two more birds on thirteen and fourteen. We got to eighteen hole, and the crowd was huge, like twenty deep along the ropes. I pounded a drive, then put it to about twelve feet from the cup. Greg two putts for par."

"What did Greg end up shooting?" Mac asked.

"Even par, 72. Pretty great with everything that was going on that day. I think Greg enjoyed watching us more than playing. Golf was the last thing on his mind. He was a cool dude."

"So then it was my turn to putt. I started lining up my twelve-footer for birdie, and all of a sudden, for the first time all day, Ava came over to help me. She went behind me, got on her knees, then gazed between my legs at the ball. I looked down and just laughed."

"What do you think?" I asked.

"I think—," she said, squinting now. "Well, I think—. Umm. You know what? I think you should hit the ball in the hole."

"I couldn't believe it. From the mouths of babes. It was so precious. Then I felt something come over me. An instant focus. I wanted this one. I lined it up, calmly pulled the putter back and drained it. The place went nuts, then Ava jumped into my arms again. I put her on my shoulders, and we waved goodbye to everybody. I swear, you could almost feel a sadness from the crowd, like they didn't want it to end. After taking Ava down off my shoulders, I told her to go give Greg a hug. She jumped into his arms, and he almost started crying again.

"This is the greatest day of my golfing life," Greg said, taking off his hat and shaking my hand. "Thank you for letting me be a part of all this."

"Greg, I don't think I've ever learned more about being a man than by watching you and how you handled yourself over the past two days. I'm proud to know you. I hope you'll let me call you my friend."

"Friends for life, young man. Friends for life."

"I ended up shooting another 31 on the back; 62 for the day. I set the course record and ended minus eight for the tournament. I was in fourth place, three shots back of the leader."

Chapter 21

The Lonely Beloved

"Ava and I walked off the putting green, turned in my scorecard, then some official told us to go to the press tent for reporters' questions. Well, I had never done an interview before, and I knew I was going to hate it. But truthfully, it ended up being pretty fun.

"They walked us into the tent, packed with reporters from everywhere. There was a table up front with two chairs for us to sit on. However, we did things our way. I sat down, and Ava hopped on my lap. I put my cap on her and told everyone that Ava would be answering all the questions for us today. So they would ask a question, I would whisper an answer in Ava's ear, and she would tell everyone what I said. Sometimes I answered seriously, but most of the time I told her a funny line. It was great. Ava loved it, laughed the whole time, and the reporters were eating it up. All of a sudden, Ava jumped out of my lap.

"Mommy!" she yelled and ran into her mother's arms in the middle of the room.

"They hugged and cried, then they walked toward my table. I stood up, having no idea what was about to happen."

"He's going to live," Ava's mother said. "Gary is going to be alright. He's got a long, hard road ahead of him, but my Gary is alive."

"That's great," Travis said. "I'm sorry that I couldn't do more. I've never felt more inadequate."

"You were amazing," she said, starting to cry. "If I hadn't ridden with Gary in the ambulance, he might not be here today. You helped save his life, and you cared for my daughter. I'll never be able to repay you. Thank you so much."

"She hugged me, kissed my cheek, then started walking away with Ava. Then Ava stopped, ran back and jumped on the table, so she could be tall enough to put my hat back on my head. Ava hugged me, then she grabbed the microphone."

"Mr. Hatfield is the greatest golfer in the world!"

"When Ava and her mother left the tent, reporters wanted to ask me some more questions, but I apologized, said it had been a long day, I was completely worn out, and I needed to go home. Surprisingly, they obliged and let me go. They even gave me a standing ovation as I left.

"I stepped out of the tent, and leaning against a pole on the other side of the ropes was Raleigh, the guy from the Houston City Amateur."

"Wow, what a round," he said, gently clapping for me. "A 62 in a PGA tournament. I knew you were good, but I didn't know you were that good. And the little girl and everything. I just wanted to tell you how proud I am of you. You represented the muni-world well. Hell, I'm proud that I got second now."

"After my Thursday round, I almost wished you had won the Amateur instead of me. I'm just glad that I didn't blow up again today. How's life, my friend?"

"Great," Raleigh said, shaking my hand. "A friend of mine is in fourth place at The Houston Open. Life couldn't be better."

"Thanks, man," I said, and then it hit me. "Hey, what are you doing tomorrow afternoon?"

"I'm gonna watch my buddy at The Houston Open. What else would I be doing?"

"Well, how about watching up close? I'm in need of a caddy, and I'd be honored if you'd carry my bag. They say it's going to be windy tomorrow, and I know that you play well in the wind. If my memory serves me, you shot two under in the wind at the City Amateur, and I'd love to have your thoughts and expertise on my bag tomorrow. I'll need you for both Saturday and Sunday, if you can do it."

"Travis, are you serious?"

"Here you go," I said, handing my golf bag to him. "I'll pick you up tomorrow morning at Memorial Park, around 9:00 am. That way you don't have to worry about the tournament parking."

"I'll wash the heads and grips tonight," Raleigh said, carefully grabbing my bag. "And I'll bring some snacks for the round. How about bananas and PB&J sandwiches?"

"That would be awesome. Hey, thank you, Raleigh. You're a life-saver. I can't tell you how excited I am to have you on my bag. But I better go now."

"Travis, you're the best. Thank you for this."

"On the way home, I started to fade. I swear I had never been that mentally tired before or after in my life. As I drove back to Mac's apartment, I knew things would never be the same again, because I looked up and a news helicopter had followed me home. I turned on the TV news, even the national news, and I was everywhere. In just one afternoon, I had somehow become the most beloved golfer in the world. And with the 24-hour news cycle, it was spreading like wildfire. They kept playing Ava's mom hugging me in the reporters' tent over and over and over.

"It was crazy. All these people loved me now, but there I was, all alone in that apartment, and I just wanted to hug my girls and I couldn't."

Travis leaned back in the booth and sighed, pretty worn out from remembering and telling it all.

"I'll go cook something," Mac said, patting Travis's knee approvingly, then marching and singing toward the kitchen. "*John Jacob Jingleheimer Schmidt. His name is my name, too...*"

Ava grabbed Travis's hand and said, "Thank you. You turned the worst day of my life into the best day of my life."

Chapter 22

The Third Round

They decided to take a break. Travis headed outside and walked in the middle of the parking lot, stretching and taking some deep breaths, probably trying to sober up a little before dinner. Ava made some phone calls, told her mom that she wouldn't be home for dinner and checked in with her fiancé. Mac was still in the kitchen, making who knows what, but it smelled delicious.

"How are you doing, Travis?" Ava asked.

"Fine. Just can't wait for this to end."

"We can finish this tomorrow if you want."

"No. Let's get it done."

They both sat down again in the booth and Ava pressed record.

"Saturday. The third round. All I remember was being dead tired. I woke up and felt like I'd never slept. For the first time in my life, I almost didn't shave. I wasn't sure if I had the energy.

"I picked up Raleigh at Memorial Park and headed for the course. We parked, and I slowly eased out of the car."

"Raleigh, I'm beat. I can't believe how exhausted I am."

"No problem," he said. "I'm tired from just watching you yesterday. I can't imagine how exhausting it would've been to be you. But that's ok, because today is going to be a struggle for everyone. Their saying 25–30 mph winds from the north, 40 mph gusts, which means the course will play much longer today, but with your length, that helps us. How about we shoot for even par today? I bet that gets us close to the lead in these conditions."

"Sounds like a great plan."

"We got there early to have a good warm-up, but the wind made it difficult to figure anything out. In an attempt to save some energy, we just hung out inside and tried not to get me more tired. It was great getting to know Raleigh, just letting him talk and hearing some new stories. It was nice just to relax.

"Oh, and guess who showed up to watch on Saturday? Mac. I spotted him about twenty minutes before I teed off. I left the apartment before he woke up, so I had no idea that he had taken the weekend off and was coming. The tournament gave each player a special pass, for a wife or dad or whatever who wanted to avoid fans and walk inside the ropes, so Mac walked with us all day. He had a blast.

"The round wasn't much to talk about at all. I bunted my way around the course. I was so worn out. I just tried to stay out of trouble and not make a big number, and with Raleigh's help, it worked out. My putter was hot, thank the Lord, because I left myself seven putts from six to eight feet for par. Luckily, I only missed two. I had two bogeys and one eagle on the day, even par.

"And Raleigh was right about the wind causing havoc for the other golfers. Guys were dropping down the leaderboard like dead flies. The average score was 76. The tournament leader on Saturday shot a 78. The only guy who played well was the great Jim Ambrose, number two player in the world at the time. The guy shot a 65 in that wind. He was three shots behind me to start the day but now had a four-shot lead. So it was him and I together in the last group on Sunday.

"It's funny. I barely remember anything about that Saturday round because it was such an insignificant part of that Saturday."

"What do you mean, Travis?" Ava asked.

"Well, I was doing the press conference after the round, just answering stupid questions and trying not to mess up, when my phone started vibrating. I looked down, and it said Lexi was calling. I couldn't believe it. I asked for a moment and answered, trying to hide my voice from the microphone on the table."

"Hey, Travis. It's the love of your life. Do you remember me?"

"Hi," I said, shocked. Lexi sounded really wasted. "How ya doing? Is everything ok?"

"Well, as a matter of fact, no. Things are not ok. The police are here, and you need to come pick up the girls."

"I quickly ended the press conference, claiming a little family emergency, and rushed out of the tent. Raleigh and Mac were there waiting at the exit, wondering what was going on."

"Lexi, are the girls ok?" I asked.

"They're fine. Well, not fine. Here, talk to the nice police officer."

"Officer Alejandro Villegas got on the phone and explained that they had responded to a 911 call from Lexi's house. The nanny had called the police to say that Lexi had burned both Charlotte and Shelby with a cigarette, on the back of their hands. The nanny explained that Lexi had gotten mad at the golf tournament on television and intentionally burned the girls, that she was abusive to the girls and that the girls wanted to live with their father. The problem for the police was Lexi denied burning the girls and said the girls had burned themselves. The nanny never saw Lexi burn the girls, so not having a witness, the police asked that the girls be placed in my care while they investigated further into the matter. So Lexi was calling me to come pick up the girls so they wouldn't be placed in protective custody."

"I'll be there as soon as I can, Officer Villegas. I'm a golfer, and I'm in a—."

"I know who you are, sir, and I understand. You get here as soon as you can. We'll be here with the girls until you show up. I hear that you're in the last group tomorrow. Second place. Congratulations."

"Thank you, sir. I'll be there as soon as possible. I'm leaving the golf course right now."

"There are no words to describe my emotions at that moment. Joy. Relief. Regret. Anger. Gratitude. You name it. I headed for my car."

"Mac, I have to go pick up the girls. Can you give Raleigh a ride back to his car at Memorial Park?"

"What?" he asked, trying to keep up with me as I jogged now. "How do you get the girls?"

"I get custody of them tonight. I don't know for how long. Can we sleep at your apartment?"

"Of course! I can't believe it. I've never met them. Hey, I got sleeping bags. You guys can camp out in the living room. I'll set it all up. Is camping ok? I got some cool ideas."

"Camping is great," I said, having no idea what he was talking about at all. "Raleigh, do you mind going home with Mac? He'll drop you off at your car. Thank you again for your help today."

"No problem," Raleigh said, still lugging my clubs on his back. "Have fun tonight, and I'll drive myself tomorrow, it's no problem. Something tells me it's going to be a special day."

"It already is," I said, and sped out of the parking lot.

Chapter 23

The Transfer

"Blue and red lights bounced off of the house as I drove into Lexi's driveway. Three cop cars filled the circular drive, and two police officers stood by the open front door. I didn't notice the ambulance until after I parked, and it did make me nervous. I greeted the cops and asked where I should go. A female officer led me into the living room where my girls' hands were being tended to by a paramedic.

"They're going to be ok," the paramedic said, as the girls ran to hug me. "Shelby has a first-degree burn, but Charlotte does have a second-degree burn, close to third. Her burn may leave a scar, but not a horrible one. They're both gonna be fine."

"I missed you so much," I said, hugging them back. "Both of you. I'm glad you're ok."

"We saw you play golf on TV," Charlotte said, beaming. "You were great."

There was this slow clapping behind me, so I turned, and there was Lexi, stumbling a little as she crossed the room, looking like she'd just come back from hell.

"Our hero has arrived. All hail Travis! He can hit a ball with a stick, so we love him, and we don't even know why. Maybe it's because we're all stupid."

"I had never seen her like this. Disheveled hair, bloodshot eyes, and a crest-fallen smile, she was an ugly drunk woman who looked totally lost."

"Are you done with the girls?" I asked the paramedic.

"Yes, all done. Charlotte will need her gauze changed every twelve hours for the next ten days, along with applying a burn ointment. I can give both to you."

"Thank you, sir, for everything," I said, then turned to the girls. "Hey, why don't y'all go wait in your rooms? I'll be up there in a while. I need to talk to Mommy and the police."

"I can wait with them," a young woman said. "Hi, I'm Jenny, the nanny. I've packed a couple of bags for the girls, for when they go home with you. It's a pleasure to meet you, sir, finally. The girls have missed you, and they love you a lot. They talk about you all the time."

"Oh, shut up, you whore!" Lexi yelled. "You've never understood anything. You've been against me from the start!"

"I quit, you bitch," Jenny said, then headed up the stairs with the girls.

"I talked to Officer Villegas and insisted on no charges for Lexi, claiming she was just drunk and unhappy, that I could get her under control. They agreed to my request, but insisted on staying until Lexi calmed down. I said no problem. So Lexi and I headed outside for a talk."

"You ok?" I asked.

"No, Travis, I am not ok. The police are in my living room."

"And they won't leave until you calm down. The police officers think you're going to hurt yourself, or somebody else again."

"Hey, I never touched Charlotte. She burned herself."

"Come on, Lexi, stop it."

Lexi sighed, then said, "We were watching you play golf on TV, and the girls were getting rowdy. I told them to shut up, or I was going to turn it off. You made a putt, and Shelby went crazy. I told the little bastard '*That was it!*' and reached for the remote. Shelby put her hand on the remote and said, '*No. We're going to watch Daddy.*' Well, nobody talks to me like that in my house, so I gently touched the back of her hand with my cigarette. I mean tapped it. She cried and ran upstairs to Jenny. I looked at Charlotte, and she's just staring at me like she's Charles Manson or something. I put my cigarette in the ashtray and asked what her problem was. Charlotte walked over, picked up my cigarette and burned the back of her hand, didn't cry at all and barely flinched. The little bitch just smiled at me. Then she started fake crying and ran upstairs to Jenny. The next thing I know, cops were everywhere, and Charlotte told them that I had burned both of their hands. So I called you."

"Charlotte burned herself?" Ava asked. "Was that true?"

"It was," Travis said, finishing his drink. "I guess she couldn't take it anymore and figured a way out. Her burn was pretty bad. She must've held that cigarette down for a few seconds. It took years for that scar to fade finally.

"I got Lexi to calm down. The police were satisfied, so they left. I told Lexi that I would come by the next morning, to check on her before my round, then I drove off with the girls."

Chapter 24

The Joy

"Dinner is served," Mac said, placing an enormous tray on an adjacent table. "I made an assortment of things."

"Oh, Mac, this is too much," Ava said, looking at the two full dinner plates in front of her. Then Mac put down two more. The two appetizer plates were filled with calamari, fried zucchini, stuffed mushrooms, spinach artichoke dip, homemade bread, and a three-cheese antipasto with cured meats, fruit, and crackers. The two main course plates had three kinds of pasta, assorted marinated vegetables, steak, chicken, and Italian sausages. "It looks and smells amazing."

"Can I get some ketchup?" Travis asked sarcastically, studying his four plates.

"Philistine," Mac shot back at him. "I'll get you a couple of Jacks, and for you, my beautiful lady, I will make you my famous Bellini."

"Oh, my gosh," Ava said, sampling each plate. "I can die now."

"I just hope we get dessert," Travis said, attacking his plates.

Mac came back with the drinks and sat down again. Travis and Ava tried to listen to Mac as he talked about each dish, but mostly, they just devoured the feast.

"So where are you guys in the story now?" Mac asked.

"The first night at your apartment with the girls," Travis said, accidentally dropping a sausage.

"No way," Mac said. "That was a great night. Hey, you're eating. Can I tell it?"

"Be my guest."

"Cool. Travis goes to pick up the girls, so I raced home to get my apartment ready for them. Thank God Travis took forever to get back. I got it looking amazing. I finished with everything, started cooking in the kitchen, when, out of nowhere, they walked through the front door.

"The girls were blown away. I had moved all the furniture out the living room so I could pitch my camping tent, inside the apartment, with three cots inside the tent, topped with sleeping bags. At the front of the tent, I had four lawn chairs surrounding a fake fire. I got three or four logs and put them on top of some red Christmas tree lights, so it glowed. The fire ended up looking pretty cool if I do say so myself. I brought in my potted plants, like ferns, philodendrons and Ficus trees, so my living room was transformed into a tropical jungle/safari type thing."

"It was cool," Travis said, in between bites. "The girls were in heaven. They forgot about me and started playing with Mac. I went to take a shower, and when I got back, they were all sitting around the fake fire, wearing Indian war paint on their faces, even Mac, eating hot dogs, Mac and cheese, and s'mores. He had known them for thirty minutes, and they already loved him more than me."

"We went to make hot chocolate in the kitchen," Mac continued, "when I look at the tent and Travis was already asleep. So we finished our cocoa, then I pushed the cots together on either side of Travis so that the girls could sleep next to him in their sleeping bags. I didn't make them bathe or brush their teeth, so they loved me."

"I woke up the next morning around 6:30 am," Travis interrupts, "alone in the tent, so I looked in the kitchen, and the girls were cooking with Mac. They were eating pancakes with strawberries, chocolate syrup, and whipped cream. Poor little Shelby's face was covered with old war paint, chocolate and whip cream."

"Travis looked at us and asked, '*Did y'all even go to bed?*'" Mac said, laughing now. "It was awesome. The girls finished eating, then Travis made them bathe and change clothes. Travis changed for the tournament and headed for the door."

"Are y'all going to be ok?" Travis asked.

"Yeah, they'll be fine," Mac said, hugging the girls. "We are going to put on some war paint and attack the settlers in the park.

Then we're going to come back here, make homemade ice cream and watch you win the golf tournament."

"Can you feed them a couple of vegetables, please?"

"Vegetables?" Mac asked, looking at the girls. "Do we want vegetables?"

"No!" all three yelled.

"Fine. Well at least hug your Dad."

"They ran over and hugged him," Mac said. "Charlotte whispered something in Travis's ear. What was it?"

"She asked me to come home quick," Travis said. "It's funny. They didn't care about me winning the golf tournament, and neither did I anymore. My whole reason for playing was gone. I had my girls now. I just wanted to stay home and play with them. But I had to leave, and I did.

"So I drive off to check on Lexi."

Chapter 25

You're Welcome

"I parked in Lexi's driveway and went to knock on the front door, but it opened before I could reach it. There stood Lexi in the doorway, perfect hair and make-up, a knowing smile, wearing a skimpy, gold silk teddy, with a matching gold silk robe that barely clung to her shoulders."

"Howdy, slugger. Ready for your big day?"

"Ready as I'll ever be. You look like you're feeling better."

"I feel perfect. I'd feel even more perfect if that police officer wasn't parked in front of my house."

"Well, that's for me. I asked Officer Villegas to meet me here this morning so no one wouldn't misinterpret my little check on you."

"You're scared of me," Lexi laughed, as her robe gently slid off her body and onto the floor. "How adorable. I saw Mac with you on television yesterday. How's he doing?"

"He's fine. Well, wish me luck."

"Oh, Travis, you don't need luck," she said, inching toward me. "You're not a child anymore. I've made you a man."

"Oh, really?"

"Yes, really," Lexi said, placing her hands lightly on his hips. "You were talented when I first met you, but you had no focus. No drive. No meaning. You did things because you liked them. Now you do things because you cherish them. I gave that to you, and you've never even said thank you once. And you know why? Because you don't want to admit that I've given you everything that now matters to you in your life."

"And what is that, Lexi?"

"Power and love," she said, her hands on his chest now. "You can do anything and dominate now, and it's because you have power. The power that comes through sacrifice, through discipline, and through regret. My Travis is unflappable and unstoppable, and you're welcome.

"Oh, and love, yes, love. I made you understand what true love is. I made you a loving father, even to another man's bastard. I forced you to love me, even when there was no love for you in return. And how do you repay me? By choosing to use your newfound understanding of power and love to play a child's game. You might as well spit in my face. You're the great love of my life, Travis, but you make me want to take it all away from you. Maybe I'll let you play today, but never again."

"I thank you for my children, but I can't deal with this anymore. I tried to make us work, and you gave me nothing in return."

"I gave you power," she said, gently clutching his face.

"Maybe, in your mind," Travis said, pushing her hands away and taking a step back, "but I didn't want it. And you never gave me love."

"Oh, Travis," she said, laughing again. "You have no idea what love is. It's a tool, my love. A weakness. If you ever really saw love, you'd miss it. Love isn't forever, Travis. Love is just a toy a child opens on Christmas morning, that breaks by noon." She laughed passionately at the sky, then composed herself. "I guess I'm not finished with you yet, am I? You don't understand that I'm allowing you to play in this silly tournament today, that I could end all this nonsense, right now. That I probably should, but I love you too damn much."

"Goodbye, Lexi," I said, walking away.

"Have fun."

"Goodbye."

"She yelled some other stuff as I left, but I didn't want to listen anymore. I had the girls, they were safe, and that was all that mattered to me. I headed to Officer Villegas' car and thanked him for coming by this morning. He asked how Lexi was and I said she seemed ok, definitely better than last night.

"So we both drove away."

Chapter 26

———◆———

The Final Round

"Sunday at The Houston Open. The Final Round, in second place, four shots back. I got there a couple of hours early. Man, I felt great. All the fatigue from yesterday was gone, and I couldn't wait to tee off. I headed for the putting green and Raleigh was already there, waiting for me.

"Morning, Raleigh. Good to see you, my friend. How was the parking?"

"No problem. I got here two hours ago. I haven't been this excited about anything in a long while."

"Your advice for yesterday was spot on. Any thoughts for today?"

"Today is our day," Raleigh said. "Jim Ambrose had a great day yesterday, but it's tough to have back to back low rounds, even if you're number two in the world. We should just play solid golf, let him blow up, and then we can mow him down. How's that sound?"

"That sounds awesome," Travis said, tapping knuckles with his caddy. "From your mouth to God's ears."

"I putted a little, but had so much nervous energy, I decided to head straight to the range and pound some balls. My ball striking was great. The contact was clean. But my adrenaline was flowing uncontrollably, so I was having a little problem with my distance control. I got excited with a nine iron and hit one ball to the 190-yard marker. But I slowed my mind down and the control came back. I developed a good rhythm. However, I resolved myself to the fact that adrenaline was going to be a big issue for me today. I went to putt a few again, and my speed was perfect. The putter felt great.

"We head to the first tee and surrounding almost the whole tee box were all my Memorial Park buddies, about fifty of them, all wearing t-shirts that said '*Travis Hatfield's Muni-Mob*.' I slapped all their hands and thanked them. Raleigh loved it.

"Then Jim Ambrose arrived on the tee. You know, it's always funny seeing somebody in person that you've only seen on television. They always look smaller, and for some reason, you feel like you already know them. I just walked up to Jim like we were old buddies, but he didn't want any of that.

"Hey, Jim. Travis Hatfield. It is a real pleasure to meet you and play with you today."

"Play well," he answered, shaking my hand briskly and not listening.

"So they announced my name, I teed off first and nailed one deep down the left side. My home crowd went nuts, cheering, hooting and hollering. But before the noise stopped and as his name was announced, Jim teed it up and proceeded to pound one down the middle, unfazed by all of the commotion. I think he was sending me a message that the noise wouldn't bother him today. What a man.

"The Sunday pins were really difficult all day, tucked behind traps or next to false fronts on almost every hole. I had never seen anything like it. Jim and I par the first five holes, just trying to manage our games and not give anything away, because players were falling down the leaderboard again for the second day, going for pins and making big numbers. Hell, watching the scoreboard and how guys were blowing up, it shook you up. But not Jim. He had a four-shot lead.

"Out of nowhere, Jim birdied the sixth hole. His approach shot was genius, six inches from the cup. I came back with a birdie on the par five eighth hole, but he rolled a birdie right back on top of me there, so I gained nothing. And adding to my misery, Jim drained a 45-footer for birdie on the ninth hole. Jim knew it was good with ten feet to go and just started walking away, knowing his caddy would pick it up, not even watching as it fell in the hole. Even I clapped.

"So after nine holes, Jim was up on me by six at −14. He didn't need to worry about noise anymore because my fans were pretty quiet, hoping I would do something, anything, and I started feeling a noose tighten around my neck, as far as winning the golf tournament went. We walked to the tenth tee, and Raleigh had this big smile."

"What are you so happy about?" he asked, a little annoyed.

"Jim Ambrose still won't talk to you. The second-ranked player in the world is scared of you cuz he knows you can still beat him, and he has a six-stroke lead. How cool is that?"

"I glanced over at Jim, and son of a gun, he did look a little nervous. Sometimes a big lead was more stressful than a one-stroke lead, and Jim seemed a little out of sorts. I don't know if Raleigh was just blowing smoke and trying to motivate me or what, but his short pep talk worked. It may sound crazy, but for the first time all day, I felt like I could win the tournament.

"So what do you think?" I asked.

"Jim's gonna try and par all the way home," Raleigh said, covering his mouth now. "Let's put a little pressure on him and see how he reacts. If Jim cracks, we will get him. If he doesn't, oh well, we get second. We're gods either way."

"I started laughing, bumped knuckles with my caddy and went for it. On the tenth hole, I barely missed birdie. The putt went right where I wanted, just didn't fall.

"Then came the par five eleventh hole, a hole that I had eagled twice already during the tournament. I pound a drive over the trees and leave myself 205 yards to the hole. I hit a six iron right at the pin, but adrenaline made it go long, and I had a 30-footer left for eagle. I hit my line on the putt, but it never broke left for me. I tapped in for birdie to cut the lead to five strokes.

"Then came the eleventh hole, a long par 4, like 490 yards, into the wind. There were some traps on the right side of the fairway, about 285 yards to carry them, and if you could hit it over them, it gave you the best angle to approach the green. However, into the wind, carrying a ball 285 yards was a mother. But hell, I had to go for it. I took a deep breath, set up and pounded it at the traps. It felt great, just carried the traps, and rolled out of view.

"I handed my driver to Raleigh and turned to watch Jim hit, but he was still talking to his caddy about their options. Out of nowhere, he grabbed a three wood. He didn't want to challenge the traps, so he was going to hit a low stringer to the left side of the fairway.

"Raleigh jabbed me in my ribs with his elbow. We both knew this was a big moment.

"Jim made a good swing, but the wind turned the ball more left than he wanted. The ball rolled out of the fairway and into the second cut of rough.

"We watched as Jim took a look at his ball, about 220 yards out and the lie was iffy. Only half the ball was visible, and there was a clump of grass right behind it. Jim and his caddy talked for a second, and then Jim pulled out a four iron. He decided to go for it. Jim took a big rip at it, but he thinned it. The ball flew like a bullet toward the green, never got more than ten yards up in the air. It landed forty feet short of the green, shot left and buried under the top lip of a greenside bunker, barely visible."

"I cannot believe he just did that," Travis said to Raleigh, as they walked to their ball. "It makes no sense. He has a five-shot lead."

"Maybe that's why he's not the first best player in the world," Raleigh said, and we both tried not to laugh.

"We finally saw my ball, and it was crazy. It must've landed on the back of the traps perfectly and raced way down the fairway. I had only 167 yards left. The pin was tucked near the front-right side of the green. A real sucker pin with the false front."

"Can you stop an eight iron on that plateau near the pin?" Raleigh asked, worried about the wind.

"No," Travis said. "It's got to be a pitching wedge, and my adrenaline is flowing right now. Let's try it."

"I reached back a little and sent the ball over the pin, spinning it back to about three feet. A sure birdie. The roar was so loud.

"Jim saw his lie in the bunker and threw his hat on the ground. Buried, about six inches under the lip. He decided to try and hit it sideways, but it hit the grass edge, stayed in the trap and rolled back down into his footprint, still on the upslope. He was lucky the ball didn't touch him. Jim walked out of the trap, regrouped for a minute, then lined it up at the pin. Raleigh and I look at each other, thinking he could leave it in that trap again. The guy took a massive rip, and it flies out, so gentle, and stops ten feet above the pin. To this day, it might be the greatest shot I've ever seen. I could not believe he got it out of that broad footprint and over that lip. I would've just cried and run away.

"Jim put a good stroke on the putt, but he missed it on the pro side and ended up making double. I drained my three-foot birdie, and now I was only down by two. The Muni-Mob went nuts. The whole place did."

"Ok, now you have to catch him," Raleigh said, as they walked to thirteen. "He's gonna par the rest. He won't take another chance. We got six holes left. We need two or three birdies. You can do this. It's your tournament now."

"It was a great speech by Raleigh, but truthfully, I wasn't as brave as my caddy. I was hoping Jim would continue to blow up. I played it safe on the next three holes and made pars, but so did Jim. Now I had to go for it.

"The sixteenth hole was a 157-yard, island par three, really skinny and long, surrounded by water, with wind crossing out of the left. Perfect to hold my draw. I hit first, chose a 3/4 pitching wedge. I made a real smooth pass at the ball and hit it just right. The ball landed on a hill in the middle of the green, then gently spun left down toward the pin, seven feet away. The crowd was so loud that I had to quiet them for Jim. He said, '*Thank you*,' his first words to me all round. Jim fatted an eight iron, and it barely caught green. I thought it was wet.

"So he's got a 45-footer that breaks twice. Jim studied the green for a while. It was a mean putt. He stroked it, on a good line, but it caught a slope and rolled ten feet by the hole. It was still his turn. He stroked it again, but it missed low. Jim three-putted, made bogey, so if I made my birdie putt, we were tied.

"I started looking at my seven-footer, and it was a beast also. It broke right, but I had no idea how much."

"What do you see, Raleigh?"

He got down behind it, then said, "A foot left, maybe more. What do you see?"

"No clue."

"I tried it a foot outside left, but it broke two feet, from seven feet! I tapped in for par, and I was only one stroke back now."

Travis sipped his Jack and Sprite Zero, then took a deep breath.

"According to the police report, at about the same time that we finished the sixteenth hole, Lexi walked out of her backdoor, wearing a white evening gown and carrying a short-barreled, twelve-gauge shotgun. A next-door neighbor, a guy named Drew, was working in his garden when he saw her."

"Everything ok, Lexi?" Drew asked.

"Everything is glorious."

"You look great."

"Well, thank you," she said, placing the shotgun on the passenger seat and hopping in her Mercedes. "Love the shirt!"

"Thanks," he said, waving as she drove off.

"The police report said Drew was wearing a t-shirt with '*I Pooped Today*' on it.

"Anyway. So we both par the seventeenth and I was still down by one stroke. I have to birdie eighteen, or it was over. We walked onto the eighteenth tee box and who did I see? You. Little Ava. You ran over, gave me a little hug and asked me to sign your program. Your mom was so mad. I signed it for you, even put my phone number down in case you ever needed anything, gave you another hug, then you disappeared back behind the ropes. You were so excited and happy like you knew I was going to birdie and eventually win. All my nerves disappeared. I wanted to win now.

"The eighteenth was a 450-yard par 4, with water all along the right side of the fairway. I spanked a drive down the right side, perfect position for the back-left pin. Jim played it safe, hitting it down the left side, away from the water. He hit his approach shot in the middle of the green, safer than safe.

"I had 109 yards. The pin was way back there on the left."

"What ya thinking?" Raleigh asked.

"I can punch a gap wedge back there," Travis said, trying to picture a shot in my mind. Then it hit him. "Give me the lob wedge."

"You sure?" Raleigh asked.

"Yeah. Let's end it right here."

"I took a big rip, trying to pinch the ball real close, so it would spin when it landed. The ball jumped so high, flying right over the pin and into the intermediate rough behind the green.

"Then it started to spin back, gently climbing onto the green, slowly tracking toward the hole. I remember Raleigh saying '*No way*.' The crowd began to roar as it got closer and closer.

"But suddenly, inches from going in, the ball swerved left and barely missed the cup. Now all I had was a two-footer up the hill for birdie."

"You called that shot?" Ava asked. "You tried to make it?"

"I think I scared Raleigh a little," Travis said, cracking a smile. "So Jim two-putts for par, I made my birdie. We were tied, and it was playoff time. Jim didn't even shake my hand after the round. He wasn't about to let his guard down with the thousands of people on the course, and millions at home watching television, all hoping he would choke and I would win. The guy was a pro and knew how to handle things."

Travis motioned to Mac for another round of drinks. They were already on Mac's tray.

"The playoff started at 5:18 pm. At 5:20 pm, Lexi walked into Marco's Restaurant, told the bartender that she was supposed to go to Mac's house for dinner but had lost his address. The bartender happily told her Mac's address and apartment number."

"Stupid idiot," Mac said, dropping off another round and sitting down again.

"The playoff went back to the eighteenth hole," Travis continued. "We drew numbers from a hat, to see who would hit first. I picked the number one, so it was my honor. They silenced the crowd, then I drilled one down the right side again, further this time, leaving myself only 94 yards. The gallery went ballistic.

"Jim teed it up, while the crowd was still cheering, barely aimed and pumped one down the right also. Perfect. It took a few bounces, rolled for a while, but abruptly stopped all of a sudden and disappeared. Raleigh and I glanced at each other, a little puzzled. Jim didn't flinch. He gave his caddy his driver and calmly marched down the fairway.

"Jim saw his ball first and threw up his hands in anguish. The ball had hit the top end of a poorly repaired divot. Whoever fixed that divot hadn't used enough sand on the top of it, and the ball fell into the gap. Jim composed himself and started discussing his options with his caddy.

"I walked up and asked for a ruling from the officials. It wasn't fair. Jim piped a perfect drive, and there was no excuse for a badly repaired divot. The golf ball was an inch deep with sand right behind his ball."

"Travis, it's ok," Jim said. "Don't worry about it."

"So I backed off, not wanting to bother my opponent. Jim pulled out a six iron, took a few deep breaths, then tried to punch it out of the divot hole. The ball shot right and dove into the water, about twenty yards right of where my drive ended up.

"It wasn't fair. Worst of all, the crowd erupted with cheers as it splashed. We got to my ball, and I couldn't take it anymore."

"Give me an eight iron," I said.

"Travis, you're 94 yards out," Raleigh said, confused. "What shot do you see with an eight iron?"

"I can't win this way."

"I don't understand."

"I grabbed the eight iron out of the bag and asked the officials where Jim's ball entered the water. We figured out the place, so I lined up and punched a little eight iron into the water, right where Jim's ball crossed the hazard. The thing that I really remember was the gasp from the crowd. Jim's first reaction was anger."

"What the hell is going on?"

"We're both hitting our fourth shot now," I said.

"Hey, I don't need your charity."

"And I don't want to win because of an unfair lie," I answered, sternly. "I want your best, not bad luck. So relax and get ready to hit. I'm gonna try and beat you, fair and square. You are too good a golfer and too fine a champion to lose because of a bad divot repair on a drive in the middle of the fairway. I have watched you for years, admired what you've done for the game and others, and I'm not going to beat you on a technicality. I can't win that way. I won't win that way. I'd rather lose."

Jim chuckled and asked Raleigh, "Is he for real?"

"He's the best," Raleigh said, proudly.

"Well, I'll be damned," Jim said and stuck out his hand. "Ok. I'll give you my best."

"I shook his hand, then we even half-hugged. The crowd cheered, and I still don't know if they knew why.

"The officials showed us our drop area, in thick rough, 102 yards out. Jim was deemed to hit first. He took a drop, and the ball disappeared in the long grass. He pulled out a sand wedge, pitched it on the front of the green, and it gently rolled all the way across, stopping below the hole, six feet away. Jim judged the rough perfectly.

"I took my drop, lined up my lob wedge and clipped it just like I wanted, flying the ball high and checking it a foot from the hole.

"But then it spun backward. Out of that rough, it spun. I couldn't believe it. It started rolling one foot, three feet, eight feet back, then it hit a slope and shot down the hill. It ended up thirty-eight feet away."

"What happened?" Ava asked.

"I hit it too well," Travis said, shrugging his shoulders. "I clipped it so well it spun, out of three-inch rough. Plus I made a poor decision in carrying the ball so far in the air. Jim hit the correct shot. I didn't.

"That was when my doorbell rang," Mac interrupted, ominously. "The girls and I were playing in the kitchen and watching the golf. I think we were baking cookies. I'm trying to figure out what was going on with Travis on that eighteenth green, when the doorbell rang. I had a hot Latin neighbor, long-legged chick, that came over every once in a while on Sundays, and I hoped it was her. I wanted to show off the girls.

"I opened the door, and there stood Lexi, in a white dress, all dolled-up, with a shotgun in her hands and a shit-eating grin on her face. I stepped back a little, afraid to even speak. Then the girls came over, screaming, and grabbing my legs. Lexi saw how petrified we were, and I swear, she started laughing."

"Is Grizzly Adams your interior decorator, Mac?" Lexi asked, gazing awkwardly at the tent and fake fire in the middle of living room.

Lexi pumped the shotgun, placed the muzzle under her chin, and smiled at her girls.

"Oh, the things we do for love," she said.

"Then she closed her eyes, pulled the trigger and blew out the back of her skull," Mac said, shaking his head. "Shelby and I were in shock. That little girl had a death grip on my left leg, and I couldn't move. But then I felt Charlotte let go of my other leg. Charlotte calmly walked to the front door, took a quick peek at what was left of Lexi on the outside door step, then slammed the front door shut."

"Let's watch Daddy," Charlotte said, sitting down in front of the TV.

"I'm gonna go finish the dishes," Mac said, trying to shake the memory out of his head and walking away.

Grabbing Travis's Jack and Sprite Zero, Ava stole a considerable mouthful, trying to quiet her nerves after Mac's account of horror. She placed the chilled glass against her forehead and took a few deep breaths.

"It helps, doesn't it," Travis said, gently inspecting her, then recognizing that she was all right. "There was nothing anyone could do, Ava. It was what Lexi wanted. If you try to understand it all, you'll go crazy. I promise. You're ok, right?"

"Yeah," Ava said. "Now I understand why you never told anyone."

"Anyway," Travis said, not wanting to dwell on things, "Jim and I were putting for bogey on the first playoff hole. I was thirty-eight feet away, and Jim was six feet away with a can-a-corn, straight uphill putt. So I had to make my putt to tie him, most likely. I lined it up, stroked it the way I wanted to roll it, but I left it a foot short, dead in the cup. I putted out for my double. The crowd gave me an enormous ovation, it went on for a while, but I silenced them so Jim could putt.

"Jim bent down to align his ball, but stopped, then glanced at me. I smiled and mouthed, '*I want your best.*' He shook his head in acknowledgment. Jim lined up his bogey putt, stroked it firmly, and the ball dropped, dead center in the cup. Jim Ambrose won The Houston Open.

"The crowd didn't cheer at first. It was more of a gasp. I started clapping and urged the crowd to join me. After a few seconds, everyone rose to their feet and cheered for Jim.

"Jim and I finished all the official stuff and the trophy ceremony, then we headed for the reporters' tent. The winner always got interviewed last, but Jim asked to go before me. I said sure.

"During his whole press conference, all he would talk about was my decision during the playoff to hit my ball in the water. Every time they tried to ask Jim about his win, all he would do was talk about what a gentleman I was and how much I had taught him about golf. The guy was amazing."

"When I lined up my bogey putt during the playoff," Jim said, "everything in my body said to miss it intentionally, so Travis and I could play another playoff hole without controversy. But then I realized that no one would remember his great act of kindness if I missed that putt. So all of a sudden, I no longer had the pressure of winning a golf tournament on that putt. Instead, I had the pressure of trying to make that putt so the world would truly know and remember what a great man Travis Hatfield is. Just think, in twenty years, no one will remember that Jim Ambrose won The Houston Open. But everyone will always remember Travis Hatfield. He did more in one weekend to make golf a better sport than I'll ever do in my whole career. He's a spectacular addition to the PGA Tour, and I hope to play with him again soon."

"Anyway," Travis continued, "Jim left, and I sat down, started answering questions, when I spot Officer Alejandro Villegas, the policeman at Lexi's house that morning, in the back of the tent. We made eye contact, and I knew something was wrong. I apologized, thanked the reporters and ran to him."

"Your girls and your friend, Mac Reynolds, are fine," Officer Villegas said. "But you need to come with me."

Chapter 27

The Truth

"The scene at Mac's apartment was horrific. They had already removed Lexi's body, but blood was still everywhere. There was no doubt in it being a suicide, but the detectives couldn't figure out the scene. They all wanted to know why she did it at the apartment, in front of the girls, and not at home. I tried to explain it to them, but they couldn't understand."

"Why did she kill herself in front of the girls?" Ava asked.

"Because she wanted to show the girls how much she loved them, and me. She was willing to die for us so we could be happy."

"That makes no sense, Travis."

"Right," he said, acknowledging the absurdity of it all. "Lexi was a troubled woman, a control freak, with no idea how to deal with us or others. Her greatest quality was her ability to manipulate others, but it was also her greatest weakness because she couldn't let anybody in her world, especially the ones she truly loved. We were her greatest weakness, in her mind, and she wanted to be close to us, but she just couldn't without giving up her soul. So she killed herself so we could be happy."

"Does what you just said make sense to you?"

"It's all I have, Ava. It's all I can come up with to make sense of it all.

"The funeral was on Thursday, and we buried her in an unmarked grave so that it wouldn't be vandalized. The only thing on her tombstone was a few lines from a poem:

'Alas, the wretched children!
They are seeking death in life, as best to have!

They are binding up their hearts away from breaking,
With a cerement from the grave.'"

"Is that what she quoted the night you met her at Marcos?" Ava asked. "Is that the poem you guessed?"

"Yeah. Elizabeth Barrett."

"What does it mean, Travis?"

"It means someone destroyed her in some way as a child and killed her soul, making her feel dead inside for life. It was her excuse for what she was and had become.

"It was why she didn't want me to play golf. She felt like I was just a child, like she used to be, and would get hurt in the end by others. Lexi truly wanted to protect me from what had happened to her. She just couldn't love me or be my friend, because she was too far gone. She loved our life together and thought that I didn't appreciate all that she had done for me, and she couldn't understand why I was always unhappy. In some ways, she was probably right."

"What could you have done differently?" Ava asked. "Can you think of anything that would've stopped her?"

"Yeah. I could've said no to playing in that scramble, the Houston Amateur, and The Houston Open. I could've sucked it up, gone home and not endangered my children. We had a good life, and I basically killed Lexi by playing golf again." Travis took a big swig of his drink. "Who knows? Maybe Lexi would've changed over the years and ended up being a great mom, and wife. Now my girls don't have a mother, and we'll never know. I never gave Lexi a chance, and it was my job to protect her. I failed her as a husband. I never should've played golf again."

"Oh, my God," Ava said. "You still love her?"

"She was my wife."

Chapter 28

The Aftermath

"Lexi left me everything. She amassed a fortune of over twenty million dollars. I had no idea. So the girls and I had a great life together. Or the best that we could under the circumstances.

"We had a tough time being close after Lexi died. Every time we looked at each other, we'd see Lexi, recalling all those memories. Still happens today, even over the phone. I think that's why we aren't very close.

"The press hounded me for years, wanting the big scoop on Lexi and the mysterious suicide. I decided just to ignore them and didn't care what they said about me. But I never realized that they would go after my daughters when they left home. I sincerely regret that and hope this book does help them.

"Your father died about eight months after Lexi. Your mother was a mess, so I became your surrogate dad on the side. Teaching you golf and watching you grow is still one of my greatest gifts in life, Ava. I don't think I'd be here today if I hadn't met you. You kept me going in more ways than you will ever know.

"I never played professional golf again. The PGA Tour wasn't my world. Too many bogus rules and stuff for me. Plus, nothing could live up to that Houston Open experience, and I'd also have to answer a lot of questions about Lexi if I played again. I wasn't about to do that. In the end, Lexi did make it so I could never play on tour ever again like she wanted. So I just went back to playing at Memorial Park, hanging out with my buddies and being a muni-guy.

"When my girls left for college, I traveled around for a year or so, trying to grieve and figure out who I was now finally, then I came back to Houston and went into the restaurant business with Mac.

I'm the '*T*' in '*T-Mac Restaurants*.' I converted the upstairs of this restaurant into an apartment, the second floor you asked about earlier. We're less than half a mile from Memorial Park, so I just walk to play golf in the mornings. At night, I hang out with Mac or just go upstairs. Don't even have a car anymore. I drink too much now."

"That's smart, I guess," Ava said.

"Shelby married a nice guy, a professor at Rice University. He doesn't play golf, but he's a good egg. Shelby turned into a great mom. Man, she loves those kids. Two boys. They invite me over for holidays and birthdays. She came out ok."

"How's Charlotte?"

"She's had a harder time. That six months I was forced to leave affected her more than I realized. Charlotte protected Shelby from Lexi, and because of that, had a lot more time alone with Lexi over those months. Lexi tried to get in Charlotte's head, and she did, but my Charlotte is a fighter.

"You wouldn't believe Charlotte now. She is the spitting image of her mom. Every time I see her, it amazes me. Charlotte even cuts her hair the same way Lexi did. I think she tries to act a little like her mother now."

"What do you mean?" Ava asked.

"A few months ago, she called to say that a guy had asked her to marry him."

"That's great," Travis said. "Do you love him?"

"Oh, Daddy," Charlotte answered, laughing. "Love is just a toy a child opens on Christmas morning, that breaks by noon."

The End

SPECIAL THANKS

To all my readers, for their time, feedback, and support:

Scott "RV Boss" Hannen, Mark "The Maestro" Day, Dr. Robert "Magic Fingers" Chapman, Darren "The Godfather" Howard, Michael "The British Invasion" Donald, Bryan "La Machine" Grant, Steve "The Hammer" West, Ben "Sneaky Eagle" Walker, Pastor Jeff "Law and Gospel" Muchow, David "The Chosen One" Ambrose, Jim "The Ninja" Gibson, Raleigh "Evel Knievel" Jenkins, and Jim "Super Fly" Klauck.

To Scott Hannen, for putting up with me and my, well, what comes along with being my friend. You make life fun, let me be me, and for that, I thank you. Always a great time teeing it up with you, my friend. I can't imagine golf without you. You've made me a better dad and taught me how to be a good friend. Thank you. Hug Selma for me.

To Mark Day, for all your insight and wisdom, and for always keeping me going on the right path. You give to me and others, yet you expect nothing in return. You are a fantastic friend, and my life is better for having met you.

To Dr. Robert Chapman, for your passion and ability to heal others, not just as a doctor. You found your calling at a young age, and you work tirelessly to help others reach their goals in life. I'm proud to call you my friend, and I thank you for all you've done for me and others.

To Flanny, my good friend and golf buddy. Hope the book surprises you. Get ready for the Member-Guest next year. Thank you for all your help.

To Mattie and Lisa, for your support and friendship. Love you, guys. You are my idea of the perfect couple. I am so blessed by meeting y'all.

To Jenny, for your support and friendship, and for going back to school. You're going to graduate!

To Darren Howard, for not kicking me out of Houston Oaks and putting up with all my stuff. You are going to heaven, a First-Class Ticket. Love ya, Brother!

To the Scottish Boys, for always checking on how the book was doing and for dealing with all my crap. Thank you, Nick, Callum, and Jamie. *Cheers!*

To Houston Oaks, for letting me use the Legacy Room to write almost half the book.

To my dog, Shadow, for patiently sitting with me while I typed at home. Yes, he got treats.

ABOUT THE AUTHOR

Bob Killinger is a stay-at-home dad with three great kids and a dynamic wife, who all live in Houston, Texas. He is a Christian, an athlete, and a snappy dresser.

United.com/United cars